Heather Dark was born and raised in Sydney. The daughter of a journalist, Heather developed a passion for writing at an early age. She has enjoyed an extensive career as a technical writer and training presenter for some of the largest companies within Australia. She currently lives in Sydney with her husband and three children. *The Designer Wife* is her first novel.

D0885867

The Designer Wife

Heather Dark

First published by Heather Dark in 2021
This edition published in 2021 by Heather Dark

The Designer Wife

EPUB: 9781922389534
POD: 9781922389541

Cover design by Red Tally Studios

Publishing services provided by Critical Mass
www.critmassconsulting.com

For Jane

PROLOGUE

When I was little, my mother used to tell me that a woman becomes invisible to men at a certain age.

Perhaps that's why she let him commit the acts that he did. She would become visible only then, once she'd served a purpose in his agenda, and she knew the secret would forever bind him to her.

For me, age is irrelevant. I've always felt invisible, except when *he* was home.

And I feel it now as I walk through the city and as I wait to order my usual coffee in the same coffee shop on Fifth. I'm the girl you don't glance back at over your shoulder.

But I won't be ignored. No.

Just you wait; I'll demand your attention.

You'll see me.
I promise …

* * *

CHAPTER ONE

ANOUK

October 14th, 2012
Afternoon

The swish and scrape of the windshield wipers eclipse the music playing on the radio. I can just make out the taillights on the car in front, the lane markings barely visible on the road. Someone's yelling. They're angry. An explosive bang—the sound of shattering glass. Silence. A whimper. There's a whirring sound, a siren perhaps, or echoing screams ...

"Anouk," Jonathan's voice startles me awake from the all-too-familiar nightmare. "We're almost there," he says. He places a hand on my shoulder. "You OK?"

I nod with the usual reassuring smile and sit up-right to look out the car window and get my bearings. We are on a tree-lined street with magnificent houses. Jonathan flashes a smile, his eyes wide with anticipation, before he turns into the driveway of a home with an ornate wrought-iron mailbox. Pebbles crackle and grind under the tires as we pass a row of oak trees and a grand front garden blanketed in autumn leaves.

"It's perfect," I say when I see it. The Georgian home is exactly as Jonathan had described.

"Well, we are finally here," he says, parking the car. Our voices have woken Charlie; he's babbling to himself in the back of the Volvo.

"Stay there. I'll come and help you out," Jonathan says.

"I'm fine. I can get out myself," I mutter; he is still too overprotective.

"Let's take a look at our new house, Charlie," Jonathan says, lifting him out of his baby seat. He kisses him on his forehead before placing the child firmly on his hip. I grab my walking stick from beside the car seat. *Come on, get it together, Anouk!* I repeat this mantra internally as I struggle to pull myself up out of the car by holding onto the door. I'm impatient to see inside.

The house has a rustic charm; its façade is painted with a mortar wash that gives it a European vibe. I love its architecture, the two chimneys, the Palladian windows with beige shutters, and particularly the circular window at the top of the home.

I follow Jonathan to the solid wood front door as he opens it with Charlie in one hand and the key in the other. Inside, large glass lanterns hang from the high ceiling in the foyer, and the faint scent of paint lingers in the musty air. To the right of the entrance is a living room, and a study or library is to the left. Both rooms have a fireplace. Jonathan is ecstatic to finally have a home library to showcase his law and political history books along with his cherished collection of unique model cars. Just past the entrance to the living room, there is a sweeping staircase.

The stairs are impractical for a nine-month-old baby. "Jonathan, we need to get the baby safety gates out of the car," I say to him as he walks ahead of me down the hallway. I'm concerned about the stairs, given that our nine-month-old will start to walk soon.

He nods, and I follow him down the hallway to the end, where there is a sunlit galley kitchen with French doors that open out onto a patio and a generous backyard. At the rear of the yard is a small wooden cubby house positioned under an oak tree with a swing hanging from one branch. I have déjà vu when I see it. *That swing,* I think, *is just like one I had growing up.* I look at Jonathan and give him an approving smile as Charlie wriggles and squirms, trying to get out of Jonathan's grasp, eager to explore the surroundings. The home is ideal for Charlie to grow up in. Jonathan picked the house himself while I was still recovering at our apartment in New York. Although I hadn't seen it before the purchase, he had my blessing to buy it. I had no attachment to the apartment and wanted Charlie to have a backyard to play in. Besides, I can't remember our life together in New York anyway.

Jonathan's parents, Ewan and Claire, live here in Buckhead too, in an affluent part of Atlanta. Ewan has a law firm: Ewan Fowler & Associates. Since his coronary bypass operation in April, he has wanted Jonathan to take over the business so he can retire. Jonathan tells me Ewan and Claire are well known among the social elite in Atlanta. Ewan in particular has strong political connections; he was even once invited to a presidential state dinner at the White House. Jonathan thought it was important to move here so Charlie could get to know his grandparents, especially given Ewan's recent health scare.

"Come, let me show you upstairs," Jonathan says as he walks toward the staircase with Charlie still in his arms.

I pause at the bottom of the staircase and wonder how on earth I am going to live here with all these stairs. *The exercise will do you a world of good, Anouk,* I think as I propel myself up the staircase with my walking stick and pause to catch my breath when I reach the landing.

Opposite the landing is a master bedroom looking out on the front garden. It has his and hers walk-in closets and a marble en suite bathroom with a shower and spa bath. To the right and left of the master bedroom are additional bedrooms. The sunlit room on the left would be suitable for Charlie; it looks out over a pond in the garden.

Adjacent to the spare bedroom is another, narrower, set of stairs. *Great, more stairs to conquer.* These stairs lead to the attic; it is not a traditional attic that one would imagine. It's renovated, painted in a cottage white, except for the exposed wooden beams of the low ceiling. The room has an ornate circular window that looks out over an array of flowers in the garden: daisies, sunflowers, and blue daze. It could become my study perhaps—a private space. The room has a calming ambiance, and strangely, I feel safe.

I hear Jonathan talking playfully to Charlie as he carries him up the stairs to the attic. They are the spitting image of each other. Jonathan was both mom and dad to Charlie when I was in the hospital. I feel like I missed out on that special time with Charlie, and sometimes I feel envious of their bond. I gaze out the attic window, daydreaming about our future together in this house.

"So, Nouk, what do you think?" Jonathan asks.

I turn to him. "You were right. I love it."

"I think you and Charlie will be happy here. A fresh start is just what we need to put the past four months behind us," he says.

I have few friends in New York, and my relationship with my parents is nonexistent. They don't want a relationship with me, which made the move to Atlanta easy to justify. I am the CEO of Designite Fashion House in the Garment District of New York. Or so Jonathan tells me. It is a successful fashion brand, and we have prominent clients and over two hundred stores across the United States. Given my expected recovery period, Jonathan appointed one of my employees, Tom Avery, to run the business as acting CEO. Tom is my closest friend and my marketing and public relations director. Jonathan said it made complete sense for Tom to take over because he had worked there for eight years, and our staff and key clients like working with him. I still have trouble reading and writing, so heaven knows how I will ever design fashion again. I don't feel like a creative person at all. When my occupational therapist and Jonathan show me fashion magazines with pictures of my designs, I don't know how I could have possibly designed the dresses and outfits in them. It just doesn't resonate with me. Right now, I don't care for fashion at all. I like wearing faded jeans and colored T-shirts.

Jonathan kisses my cheek, bringing me back to the present.

"I agree, Jonathan. A fresh start is exactly what I need,"

I want to kiss him, but I still feel shy, awkward. We have been married for ten years, but for me, it feels like we've only been dating a few months.

"Good. I was hoping you would love it," he says.

Despite having lost all my memories of him and our years together, I knew I cared for him when I woke up in the recovery unit of the hospital and saw his face.

Many times, I've studied his facial features—the lines on his face that are starting to show his forty-one years. His hazel eyes appear pale green in the sunlight coming through the attic window, and a lone dimple appears on his right cheek when he smiles. Jonathan has stood by me throughout my recovery. Some men, perhaps, would have left. I take a mental picture of us in this moment. I want to remember this day—always.

* * *

CHAPTER TWO

ANOUK

October 15th, 2012
Morning

I awake to the sound of the moving truck doors opening with a metallic bang.

"Nouk, they're here!" Jonathan calls from downstairs.

"Coming!" I croak. *Wake up, Anouk.* I check the time on my cell phone on the floor. It's 8:00 am. *Damn, I've slept in.* I had a terrible night's sleep. I look over at the portable crib, and Charlie's not in it. *Jonathan must have him.* Last night, Charlie was unsettled in the portable crib, and Jonathan and I slept on an uncomfortable inflatable mattress that bounced me around every time Jonathan tossed and turned. Thank heavens our bed and Charlie's crib arrive today. I get dressed without showering, grab my walking stick, and meet Jonathan downstairs. He is already directing four burly men who are moving our furniture inside. He instructs them where to put what, with Charlie in his arms. Jonathan doesn't want me to exert myself too much today. He knows I still get tired.

Boxes upon boxes come inside.

"Where do you want it, lady?" one of the movers asks before I can greet my husband and baby.

"Um … What's it labeled?" I ask, rubbing my eyes.

"Anouk's wardrobe," he says gruffly. "There are thirty boxes like this."

What? Thirty?

"Oh, upstairs please," I say through a suppressed yawn.

Jonathan gives me a playful grin like he knows something that I don't. I frown at him quizzically. As charismatic as he is, I'm in no mood for his playfulness this morning.

"Jonathan, I'll start unpacking the kitchen boxes, and I'll make us some … *Come on, Anouk; find the word* … some … err … toast," I stammer.

Sometimes I just can't find my words, particularly when I'm tired, like I am this morning. The legacy of a head injury.

I need coffee. We had packed some basic food items before we left New York. One mover assists me in locating all the boxes labeled "kitchen" and helps me unpack the kitchen items. I make myself an instant coffee before I locate the French press. Jonathan likes to grind a high-quality coffee bean and then brew it. I eventually find the toaster.

After breakfast, Jonathan sets up our four-poster bed upstairs with the help of all four movers. I start unpacking my thirty boxes while Charlie crawls around me and under the clothes I lay out on the floor. Thankfully, I have a generous walk-in closet; I can't believe the amount of clothes I own. Jonathan said some of them were in storage, but I had no idea I owned this much. Now I know why Jonathan gave me that playful grin: He knew how much I had to unpack.

I wade through jewelry, evening gowns, suits in all colors and cuts, sundresses, shorts, skirts, shirts, jeans, T-shirts, belts, shoes, and hats. One by one, I hang, fold, and put them all away with lightning efficiency. *Almost done.*

There is only one box left to open. Inside is a royal blue floor-length evening dress, backless and long-sleeved, with a skew neckline. The dress is fitted from the waist down, cut to follow the contours of the body before slightly fanning out at the base. I look at its label to check the size. It's a size four. *Darn.* I'm currently a size six. I ate my way through my recovery. In the early days following the accident, all I could do in the hospital was eat, mostly from boredom, so I'm not surprised by my weight gain.

I hold the dress up to my body and go into the bathroom to look at myself in the mirror. My blue eyes look tired, and my heart-shaped face appears older than my age of thirty-five years. Thankfully, most of my two six-centimeter scars are well hidden under my hairline. They start behind my left ear and finish just under the base of my hairline at the back of my neck. The hair has started to grow back. You wouldn't know the scars are there when my hair is down. Not that I'm vain, but I'm grateful my surgeon was thoughtful enough to only shave what he needed to. I hand comb and position my shoulder-length hair over the dress so I can envisage what I would look like in it. *This one is familiar.*

"Do you remember that dress?" a voice behind me asks. I jump. Jonathan's standing in the bathroom doorway.

"Jonathan, you scared me,"

"Sorry. You wore that dress the first night we met." His voice is heavy with nostalgia.

"Really? It's stunning."

"*You* were stunning that night. You haven't worn that dress since. It's a one-off you designed for yourself."

"Please tell me about the first time we met," I ask. *I want to remember.*

"How 'bout over dinner tonight?" he says, combing my hair off my face with his long fingers.

"Sounds good. Oh, what about getting some ..." *Find the words, Anouk!* "takeout? I want Charlie in bed early; he didn't get much sleep last night," I say, reaching up to wrap an arm around Jonathan's neck. His lean frame towers over my five-foot, four-inch body.

"Done. Cooking is the last thing we will feel like doing tonight," Jonathan says.

"I've put together Charlie's crib. Why don't you have a nap when Charlie has his? I'll make you some lunch, then you need to rest," he says, kissing me on the cheek before leaving the room.

I put Charlie to bed after lunch. He falls straight to sleep, comforted by the familiarity of his crib. I take Jonathan's advice and have an afternoon nap too.

When I wake a couple of hours later, the movers are gone, and I take Charlie outside to play in the afternoon sunshine while Jonathan unpacks his boxes in our bedroom. Charlie and I crawl and roll around in the grass. He is fascinated by the color and texture of the autumn leaves, and he lets out a joyful giggle when they crunch between his chubby hands. I watch him intently, fascinated by his reactions to his new environment. I feel so blessed to have Charlie. He is a delightful child, and I adore him. He is the reason I was so determined to recover, to get out of bed each morning and do my rehabilitation exercises. He gave me a reason to get well and to live. I lie back on the grass, relishing the warmth of the autumn sun on my face as I watch Charlie explore the garden. I think I'm going to enjoy living here in Atlanta.

"What are the two of you up to?" Jonathan asks as he walks outside to join us. He scoops Charlie off the ground into his arms and spins him around.

"Nouk," he sighs. He pauses, taking in a deep breath. "There is something I've been meaning to tell you. I mean, most of it you already knew before you had the accident, but you may not recall," he says in a low and apprehensive voice. He gives Charlie a kiss on the cheek before putting him back down on the grass.

He rubs his hands together in a nervous fashion.

"My parents don't know about Charlie," Jonathan blurts out.

"What do you mean they don't know about Charlie?" I shout at him, startling Charlie.

"I never told them you were pregnant, and I didn't tell them about his birth," he says quietly.

What the … ? "Are you kidding me? Why, Jonathan?" I ask, now standing in front of him.

"I'm sorry, Anouk. I didn't want to burden you with all my family drama, but long before you had the accident, I had a falling out with Mom and Dad … about two years ago. You knew about this. They were devastated that I didn't want to move back to Atlanta.

"I explained to them that because you had your business in New York, we were staying there. They had trouble accepting that. You have to understand that ever since I was a little boy, Dad has dreamed that I would take over the family law firm. It was just an expectation he had of me—"

"But I don't understand … why didn't you tell them about Charlie?" I interrupt.

"I stopped talking to them because they were always blaming you, talking about you as though you were the reason I didn't move back to Atlanta. I just couldn't take it anymore. So, I said if they continued to disrespect my wife, I wouldn't talk to them anymore. And so that's what happened." He sighs.

"I don't want to come between you and your parents, Jonathan," I stutter.

"This had nothing to do with you. My father just had unrealistic expectations. He always did when it came to me. I mean, I only did law to keep *him* happy," he grumbles.

"I can't believe they don't know you have a son, Jonathan!"

"I don't know how to tell them. I should have told them, but I was angry with them. But then when Dad's health deteriorated after his coronary bypass in

April, Mom called me, and I was going to tell them then, but I thought Dad would get too upset, so I put it off again until he had fully recuperated. Then you had the accident, and I decided to focus on you. Us. I want them to meet Charlie. I just don't know how I'm going to break it to them now after all this time," he says, running his hands through his unruly hair in frustration.

I shake my head. "They know we moved in here yesterday. You need to call them and tell them,"

"You're right," he says with a sheepish look.

"Just do it, so they have time for it to sink in before Charlie meets them. I can't believe you didn't tell me this earlier. What if they had turned up at the door this morning? What on earth were you thinking?" I ask.

"I'm sorry. I never want to hurt you or lie to you or them," he says, placing a hand on my shoulder.

"What was my relationship like with them before you stopped contact with them?" I ask now in a soft voice, trying to hide my anger.

"You liked them, and they do like you. Like I said, though, they always thought I should have married someone in our hometown and not some New York fashion designer who would take their only son away from them," he says, letting out a quiet chuckle, and nudging me jokingly on the arm.

I roll my eyes at him. Charlie starts to grizzle and cry. "I'll get Charlie his dinner and put him to bed.

Jonathan, call your parents ... And ask them to come over at six Saturday night for dinner," I say, exasperated, before picking Charlie up off the grass.

* * *

CHAPTER THREE

ANOUK

October 15th, 2012
Evening

Charlie settles in his crib, and I go downstairs to locate Jonathan. I turn on the baby monitor in the kitchen, and then I see Jonathan standing outside in the yard, looking at the sunset, with a glass of wine in one hand and his phone by his side in the other. *He's called Ewan and Claire.*

"You OK?" I ask.

"Yeah. That was one of the toughest phone calls I have ever had to make," he says with a sigh. His eyes are glassy.

"How did they take it?" I ask, putting my arm around his shoulder despite still feeling angry at him.

He musters a smile. "They are excited to be grand-parents, but they're devastated I didn't tell them sooner. They're hurt, of course, but they can't wait to meet Charlie. Dad wants me to meet him at his office tomorrow morning to discuss taking over the business."

"How do you think they'll respond to me when they see me after all this time … Are they going to blame me?" I ask hesitantly.

"No. It's me they're upset with. They're looking forward to seeing you again," he says. "They want to help us out with Charlie. It's just going to take some time for me to make it up to them," he says, leaning over to kiss me on my cheek. "I'm really sorry, Nouk, that I didn't tell you sooner. I was protecting you," he says, heaving a sigh.

I study his eyes that are begging mine for forgive-ness, and despite the hurt I feel right now, I relent.

"I forgive you." I can never stay mad at Jonathan for long, no matter how hard I try. How can I, after everything he has done for me? After all, he's the fa-ther of my child, and the truth is I've fallen helplessly in love with him. All over again.

"So, what do you feel like for dinner?" he asks.

"Chinese."

"I'm on it," he says as he walks back into the kitchen to look up a local Chinese restaurant on his laptop.

"Jonathan, I'm going to take a bath before dinner arrives," I call out to him.

* * *

I exhale as I slide into the spa bath, close my eyes, and let the warmth of the water wash away the stress of the day. I am still reeling from the revelation that Jonathan hadn't told his parents about Charlie.

I turn on the jets in the tub, and my thoughts turn to Jonathan. Despite the hurt, he makes me feel safe, protected, and loved. I shave my legs and get out of the bath, then make my way to the walk-in closet while towel drying my hair. I find an indigo satin nightdress with a matching full-length robe. *Wear it, Anouk.* I put it on; Jonathan has only seen me wear jeans, T-shirts, and sweatpants these past four months. As I attempt to blow dry my blonde hair into some semblance of a hairstyle, the front doorbell chimes.

I mentally prepare myself before I walk down the stairs, willing my right leg to work. I don't want to use my walking stick. The faint sound of music drifts up from downstairs, getting louder as I near the kitchen; it's the pretty melody of *that* song. I can't remember its name, but he plays it often. He says it used to be our favorite song to listen to when we relaxed together with some wine after work on balmy summer nights in New York. I can see Jonathan setting the table as I approach the kitchen. I stand still in the doorway to just admire him for a few seconds, watching him prepare the dinner table with such perfection, meticulously placing the knives and forks on the table.

I gaze at his unshaven face; it's manly. He's handsome in an old-fashioned kind of way, straight out of a 1950s movie—broad-shouldered and with dark wavy hair.

"Looks good," I say, startling him.

He looks up at me and raises an eyebrow. "So do you," he says with a look of surprise. "Dinner is served, madam," he says in a posh English accent, waving his hand over the Chinese feast in front of us. He pulls out a chair for me.

"Thanks." I chuckle, taking a seat. I'm ravenous, so I immediately serve myself. Fortunately, I can still use my fork in a sophisticated, ladylike manner, although my right hand still struggles to use a knife with precision.

"So, what should I cook for your folks Saturday night?" I ask when I finish my mouthful.

"I think we should serve something special, like lobster. Dad loves it," Jonathan declares.

"Lobster?" I laugh. "A pot roast would be easier."

"I really want to serve lobster. I think my folks would appreciate it," he says before helping himself to some takeout.

"Are you serious? It's not like we're hosting a state dinner at the White House, for heaven's sake."

"Calm down, Nouk. It was just an idea," he says as he places a serving of Peking duck on his plate.

"I wouldn't have the first clue about how to cook a damn lobster," I say, exasperated.

"It's good to see you've got your feisty temper back," he says, stroking my arm in an attempt to lighten the mood.

Temper? I don't have a temper.

He continues. "We could serve it with potatoes and asparagus," he says through a mouthful of food.

I want to make Jonathan happy, so I relent. "OK, but you need to buy all the ingredients and cook it," I say.

Jonathan is an amazing home cook. In the early days after I came home from the hospital, he would cook for me every night after work. He likes to experiment with different recipes and exotic ingredients. Although I frequently offered to cook, given that I was at home all day, he would insist. He would say that cooking helps him relax after a day at the office or after being in court for hours.

He puts his knife and fork down, puts his hands under his chin, and looks reflective as he finishes chewing his last bite. "On second thought, how 'bout we just hire a personal chef, and then the problem is solved," he says, flashing me one of his charismatic smiles.

"Chef? We can't afford that!"

"Actually, we can. I mean, *you* definitely can," he chuckles.

"Don't be so extravagant. That's a waste of money," I say, waving my fork at him in disapproval.

"Well, we have done it before. Let's make it easy on ourselves, and then we can both relax with our company Saturday night," he says, shrugging his shoulders.

"Have we really hired personal chefs before?" I ask, surprised by this revelation.

"We hosted dinner parties in New York, and yes, we hired a personal chef on a couple of occasions. It never bothered you before. We're not short of a dime, Anouk," he says matter-of-factly.

What? Although I knew we were comfortable financially, I had never really given it much thought, but I guess I would have money if my company is as successful as Jonathan always tells me. I trust Jonathan to handle my finances.

"Oh. OK," I concede without argument, now relieved that I don't have to cook.

"Let's go to the living room and have some wine," he says.

* * *

Jonathan hands me a glass of chilled Chardonnay as we take a seat on the floor in front of the fireplace.

"Jonathan, tell me about the first time we met," I suggest, staring at the flames of the fire.

"Of course. Where should I begin?" he muses, scratching his head in reflection. Then he says, "Well, we first met back in February of 2001, at New York Fashion Week. You were there showcasing your first spring collection. My friend Brad from college and his girlfriend, Sarah, invited me to attend. I had just broken up with my then-girlfriend Lauren, and I think Brad and Sarah took pity on me being single at the time. They were always inviting me out somewhere with them. Anyway, Sarah was working there in event management, and she invited Brad and me backstage, you know, for a sneak peek before the runway show started. Sarah was keen to introduce me to some of the models." He chuckles, giving me a sheepish look.

I roll my eyes at him. "Keep telling the story," I say, pushing his shoulder with my hand.

He continues. "You were backstage fitting a model into her dress, and someone knocked into me from behind. I tripped and bumped into you, knocking you onto the model you were fitting. You yelled at me, 'Hey, watch where you're walking!' I said, 'I'm sorry,' and you snapped back, 'So you should be! You nearly ripped her dress!' I didn't know who you were, but I liked your feistiness. So I said, 'How about I make it up to you over dinner?' and you replied, 'No thank you,' so I retorted 'Oh, that's right, you models don't eat.' You laughed and told me that you were, in fact, not a model. Anyway, just then, Sarah called you over because it was time for your collection to get on the runway. Brad and I watched from the front row.

"When you walked the runway at the end of your collection preview—to raucous applause, I might add—you glanced at me. You had on that royal blue dress, and I smiled at you, but you didn't return my smile, much to my disappointment. So I went back-stage and offered to take you to dinner again. You said, 'I don't go to dinner with strangers.' But then Sarah came over to congratulate you on your collection, and she introduced me to you. She said, 'Jonathan, this is Anouk Jackson. Anouk, this is Jonathan Fowler; he's a good friend of my boyfriend, Brad.'

"I said 'Anouk, it's a pleasure to meet you. Now will you join me for dinner? I'm no longer a stranger,' and you agreed. We went to dinner at a French bistro downtown and talked for hours. I fell in love with you that night," he says stroking my face.

He pauses momentarily, studying my face before kissing me softly on the cheek.

Hmm ... He smells good. His cologne is earthy and woody, with notes of sandalwood and lavender. His lips are now on mine. *Oh my.* I kiss him back, wrapping my arms around his shoulders. He lays me down and kisses my neck. I feel one of his hands at my waist, undoing the bow on my robe. I stop his hand. *I'm nervous.*

"Jonathan, I—"

He whispers in my ear before I can finish my sentence. "Trust me," he says.

It's the first time we have made love for as long as I can remember.

***

CHAPTER FOUR

ANOUK

October 16th, 2012
Morning

I can hear crying. Someone's yelling from the dark. I can't make out the words through the sound of the hammering rain. An explosive bang, the sound of shattering glass. Blackness. My head is filled with whirring sounds, and pain envelopes my body. Help! I can't breathe ...

I wake up, breathless, to the sound of a baby's cry. I sit upright, disoriented, and a wave of panic washes over me. *Oh my god; it's Charlie.* I can hear Jonathan's faint snore next to me as I reach for my cell phone on the bedside table to check the time; it's 5:00 a.m. I limp down the hall to Charlie's room, and he's standing in his crib, red-faced, with tears stream-ing down his chubby cheeks. His hazel eyes widen with relief when he sees me. I pick him up and hold him to my chest.

"I'm here," I soothe, kissing him on the top of his head and inhaling his baby smell. I rock him in my arms for a while next to his bedroom window, rel-ishing the warmth of his tiny body against mine. He stops crying. *He's OK.* Maybe he had a bad dream too. I curse myself for not waking up to Charlie sooner. I wonder how long he was crying before I finally came to him. Jonathan didn't wake up to his cries either. I swear he could sleep through anything, and I dare not think about how he got up for Charlie at night when I was in the hospital.

I glance out Charlie's bedroom window, and my eye catches the outline of a shadowy figure; someone standing in our front garden in the dark. I jolt, star-tled, causing Charlie to cry again. I look down at Charlie to soothe him, then look out the window again. It's gone. My eyes scan the front garden, but all I can see are the shadows of the moonlit trees.

It was just my imagination, and my dream made me jumpy, I reassure myself as I walk downstairs to the kitchen to make Charlie a bottle of baby formula.

* * *

At breakfast, I tell Jonathan about my dream while Charlie plays with his scrambled eggs next to us. "But it felt so real, Jonathan," I explain.

"Nouk, I'm sure it's not uncommon among trauma patients to have dreams about the traumatic event. Please book into the rehabilitation program at Emory Hospital to continue your rehabilitation therapy. Emory can get your medical files from Mount Sinai. I'll look up Emory's number for you."

He goes to his laptop and jots down a number on a piece of paper.

"Shit!" he says after looking at his watch. "I'm late. You just get booked into rehab today, OK? I'll be home at around four. I'm off to meet Dad at the office, so wish me luck," he says as he leans down to give Charlie and I each a kiss on top of the head.

"Good luck."

"Gotta go. By the way, last night was incredible," he says, flashing a broad grin before he walks out the front door.

Oh my god! My horrible dream had tarnished the memory of our lovemaking.

The autumn sun illuminates my kitchen, interrupting my thoughts of last night. It's a perfect morning to take Charlie for a walk in his stroller just before his morning nap. Besides, it will be good exercise for my right leg. I won't need my walking stick; I'll have the stroller for support. I get changed out of my night-dress and quickly change Charlie's diaper.

Outside, I push the stroller along our pebble driveway and up to where it meets the street and decide to take a left turn. It's picturesque; squirrels scamper through the autumn leaves, and humming-birds hover among the trees. The branches of the oaks lining the street meet in the middle to make a tunnel-like canopy. Charlie points at them with his chubby little fingers and squeals. He is mesmerized by the movement of the limbs swaying rhythmically with the morning breeze.

Atlanta, much to my surprise, is lush with south-ern pines, magnolias, and magnificent oaks. I can now see why Jonathan calls it a "city in a forest." I walk past a couple of homes on the left side of the street. Like so many houses in Atlanta, they are stunningly beautiful. I come to the third home on the left, a red brick 1930s Georgian home, and stop to take a look. It, too, has a pebble driveway, but this house is positioned much closer to the street than ours. I hear the sound of a car coming up be-hind me, so I move the stroller off the road just before a black Mercedes-Benz speeds into the drive-way in front of me and parks. A well-dressed, busty brunette gets out, and as she turns to lock the car, she looks up and sees me standing at the end of her driveway.

"Mornin'," she says with a wave of her hand.

"Err … morning," I rasp, clearing my throat. *Introduce yourself, Anouk.* I proceed to walk up her driveway toward her. "Hello, I'm Anouk. I've just moved into the house three doors down,"

"Oh, hello. Brianna Sperling," she says with a southern drawl, flicking her long hair out of her face. Her perfume wafts to my nose as she reaches out her right hand to shake mine.

I will my limp right arm up to shake her hand. "This is Charlie," I say, stroking his honey-blond hair. She doesn't look at Charlie at all; her eyes are firmly fixed on me. *Maybe she doesn't like kids.*

"Where have you moved from, hon?" she asks in a friendly voice.

"New York."

"Well, welcome to Westwood Street," she says. She has an inviting smile; it's framed by full red lips that highlight her perfect white teeth and porcelain skin. Up close, she is stunning. She is petite, possibly a size four. She looks my age, but she could be older; it's hard to tell.

"Thanks. How long have you lived here?"

"Oh, honey, we've been here ten years. Love the place. You look kinda familiar; have we met before?" she asks with a questioning look.

"I don't think so," I say, shaking my head. I don't recognize her.

"I know your face from somewhere. Are you on television?" she asks, frowning and smiling at the same time, one manicured finger pointing at me. She is overtly animated with her hands and facial expressions.

"Oh no. Not me," I laugh.

"I don't forget a face. What do you do for a livin'?" she asks. She talks fast and comes across as being very self-assured.

"Um … I'm a … was … I'm a fashion designer," I stutter in embarrassment. I still can't get used to the idea that I used to design, and it feels even stranger now that I have said it out loud. It doesn't help that I'm looking rather frumpy and unfashionable today, makeup-free and clad in sweatpants and sneakers, my unbrushed hair pulled back into a ponytail.

"Really? What's your name again, hon?" she asks.

"Anouk … Fowler," I say.

"Oh my," she gasps. "You don't happen to be *the* Anouk from Designite Fashion House?" Her blue eyes widen with excitement, and her mouth gapes.

"Yes, um … Why? How do you know?" I ask. *Shit. I'm not ready for these types of conversations. I must make that appointment with rehab today.*

"Honey, are you kiddin' me? Take a look at what I have on," she says loudly as she runs her hands up and down the sides of her body and does a spin on her black patent Mary Jane stilettos. She is wearing a long-sleeved, black chiffon blouse. It has a white trimmed Peter Pan collar with white buttons down the front and on the cuffs. She has matched it with a fitted, knee-length black skirt that's pleated at the base. "I'm your biggest fan!"

Oh my god. I don't recognize the design. Thankfully, Charlie starts to whine, so I use it as a cue to change the subject.

"Thank you. I really must get Charlie home for his morning nap," I say as I lean down to the stroller to stroke Charlie's forehead. I notice her gaze moves to behind my left ear. *Crap! She's noticed my scars.* I curse myself for not leaving my hair down today.

"Hey, weren't you in a car accident? I remember hearing something about it in the news," she says.

"What! Oh … I didn't know it made the news," I stutter, surprised by this revelation. *Why didn't Jonathan tell me that?*

"Come on, honey. You're well known," she says, nudging me.

Oh no.

"How ya doin', anyway?" she continues, placing a hand on my shoulder. Her simple gesture makes me relax, and I find myself wanting to talk to her for some reason. Heaven knows how long it's been since I have talked to anyone other than Jonathan.

"I'm doing OK, actually. I still have some physical challenges and memory loss, but I'm getting better each day," I explain.

Charlie starts to cry, pulling at the straps of his stroller.

"Brianna, it was lovely to meet you, but I have to … ahh … I really have to go."

"I understand. Hey, what are you doin' ten-thirty on Saturday morning? I'm having some ladies over to my place for a morning tea. I would love for you to come. I can introduce you to some of the locals," she says.

"That would be nice … maybe just for a little while."

"Great! I'll let you go so you can get your little one off to bed, and I'll look forward to it and to seeing you then." She smiles.

"Oh, what should I bring?" I ask.

"Just yourself, and bring your little one too."

"See you then." I wave as I walk back down her driveway to the street. I have a good feeling about Brianna, and she appears sincere. It's been so long since I've had female companionship, and I'll look forward to seeing her again on Saturday.

* * *

At home, I put Charlie in his crib for his morning nap, and I decide to unpack the remaining four moving boxes in the library. I want to surprise Jonathan by having all his books on the shelves when he gets home.

I find a box marked "Photo Albums," and inside are our wedding and honeymoon photo albums. There is also an album with photos of Tom, Jonathan, and me at various fashion events and parties surrounded by beautiful women in designer clothes—models, most likely.

At the bottom of the moving box is a lone photo of Jonathan and Charlie in the hospital. Charlie's a newborn, wrapped in a checkered blanket in a bassinet. Jonathan has a proud smile on his face. I turn the photo over. It's undated, but there are handwritten words on the back. It takes me a minute to read them: *My favorite boys, x.*

I must have given it to Jonathan. I rummage through other boxes and find a spare photo frame that I put the photo in, then I take it upstairs and place it on my bedside table. Then I move on to unpack my remaining box for the bathroom vanity. I find beauty products, and toiletries inside, as well as a lone pregnancy test. It still has a faint positive result marker on the stick. *Whoa*! It hits me. Déjà vu, a memory, perhaps: I'm showing Jonathan the positive result on the pregnancy test. He's not happy, and he walks away from me. *Darn.* Then it's gone. I can't wait to tell Jonathan that I can remember the moment

I told him I was pregnant, but I wonder why he appeared unhappy.

I go downstairs to make an appointment for the rehabilitation program at Emory University Hospital. I can start Friday with my physical, speech, and occupational therapy. They also want me to attend their outpatient program two days per week, so I'll need to talk to Jonathan about potentially hiring a nanny to care for Charlie on those days.

I spend the afternoon frantically cleaning, limping around the house with Charlie in one arm. There's no pleasing Charlie this afternoon. He's been grizzly ever since he woke up from his nap, and he won't let me put him down on the floor for a second or two without throwing a tantrum. I find myself feeling flustered and exhausted by his constant crying. I'm tired but decide to keep moving and start putting all the empty moving boxes into the garage, bouncing Charlie on my hip. As I bend down to pick up the last couple of empty boxes in the library, I feel it—the sense of being watched. And then I spot a dart of movement from the corner of my eye. Someone is watching from outside the library window. Hesitant, I turn to look at the window, but nobody is there. *That's odd*. Perhaps it was my imagination. But I'm sure I saw something. Curious, I carry Charlie to our front door and cautiously open it to peek outside. There is no one to be seen. Outside, I walk as quickly as I am able to our front garden, scanning it. Then I see a flash at the end of our pebble driveway, at the street, and catch a glimpse of a running figure wearing a black hooded sweatshirt. *Who was that?* I rush back into the house and lock the front door, then I move swiftly through the house, carrying Charlie, locking all the doors and windows. I try to calm my nerves by reassuring myself that I'm safe in the house as I fold laundry and stack the empty moving boxes in the garage.

"Nouk, I'm home!" Jonathan calls from the front entrance.

Thank goodness, he's home early. "I'm in here!" I call back from the garage. "Oh Jonathan, thank god you're home," I say as he greets us. He's glowing.

"You OK?" he asks, now with a look of concern as he kisses my cheek.

"No. Someone was watching me today from the library window. I'm sure of it. I mean, I sensed it, and when I went outside, I saw someone running down our driveway," I blurt.

"What? Did you see their face?" he asks surprised.

"No. I saw them from the back. They were wearing a black hooded sweatshirt."

He gives me a questioning look as though he doesn't believe me. "I wouldn't worry. Probably just teenagers mucking around."

"I have this feeling someone is watching me. I know it sounds crazy, Jonathan, but I thought I saw someone standing outside the house in the early hours this morning too."

"Please don't worry. It's safe here in Buckhead," he says, dismissively waving his hand.

He's right, and I'm starting to sound paranoid, so I nod and change the subject. "How was your first day?" I ask with an upbeat tone.

"Good. Better than expected. Dad and I had coffee together this morning. He looked well. He took me through some of his recent cases, and we met with a client. It was good to see him again. He can't wait to meet Charlie. So what did you two do today?" he asks, taking Charlie from me into one arm.

"I took Charlie for a walk in his stroller, and I met one of the neighbors a few doors down, Brianna Sperling. She's invited me to morning tea at her place on Saturday."

"Good, sweetheart. It'll be good for you to get out and meet some of the locals." He smiles.

"Guess what? I had a flashback today. A memory of us," I say, clapping my hands with excitement.

"You did?" he asks, raising his eyebrows.

"I was unpacking the box for the bathroom, and I found a pregnancy test, and when I picked it up, I remembered showing you the positive result. You weren't happy when I showed it to you, though. Why weren't you happy?" I frown.

"I was ecstatic when I found out you were pregnant," he replies, looking confused.

"You definitely appeared unhappy," I say.

"I remember the day you told me you were pregnant. It was the best day of my life," he smiles, pausing momentarily. "What I'm about to tell you may come as a surprise ... You never wanted children," he says in a quiet, hesitant voice.

"What?!" I feel a lump rise in my throat. *I don't believe it.*

He puts his hand on my arm, clears his throat, and continues. "Your career was always the priority, Anouk. I had been pressuring you for years to have children, but you were adamant that you didn't want them. When you found out you were pregnant that day, *you* were devastated. You thought it was going to ruin your career. I was unhappy because you didn't want the baby. I pleaded with you to keep the baby. And thankfully, you fell in love with Charlie when you saw him on the first ultrasound. You were so excited when you felt his first kick. You didn't want to tell anyone until you were at least twenty weeks along."

"I don't believe it, Jonathan ... I mean, I love Charlie so much. I can't imagine not wanting him," I say. Tears well up in my eyes at just the thought of my life without Charlie in it.

"It's the truth. I swear to you," he says.

Then, remembering what Brianna said, I ask, "Why didn't you tell me the accident was reported in the media?"

"What do you mean?" he asks with a frown.

"Brianna, the neighbor I met today … She told me she heard about my accident on the news."

"It was only briefly mentioned in the news. All that was reported was that you were in a car accident and were being treated in the hospital. That's all that was mentioned, so there's no need to worry about it, OK? You were in intensive care at the time. I guess I just forgot to mention it to you," he says, shrugging.

"You should have told me!"

"Why does it matter now?"

"Because I need to know these things so I'm prepared when I'm talking to people. I guess I didn't … I didn't realize that I'm well known," I sob.

"Of course you're well known. Your fashion designs are in magazines all the time. You are the CEO of the most recognized fashion brand in the United States, for heaven's sake, so people are going to recognize you! It didn't bother you before—"

"Well, it bothers me now, Jonathan!" I interrupt. "It just doesn't resonate with me. I wish I could remember. I wish I could remember who I am," I say.

Jonathan puts his briefcase down to wrap his free arm around me.

"I know it's frustrating for you. With time, your memory may come back. You must try to be patient. Have you made that appointment with the rehab center yet?"

"Yes. I start Friday for two days a week at Emory. Can you mind Charlie for a little while on Friday?"

"Sure. Now why don't you go and relax. I'll take Charlie outside," he says, wiping a tear from my cheek. "I love you," he says, kissing me on my forehead.

***

CHAPTER FIVE

ANOUK

October 17th, 2012
Morning

"I'm off to the office now, Anouk. I'll be home late!" Jonathan calls from downstairs.

"Have a good day!" I call back.

"Daddy's off to work now," I singsong to Charlie as I carry him downstairs to make him a bottle. Afterward, I put Charlie to bed for his nap, and it's not long before I'm interrupted by the chime of the front doorbell. I go downstairs and look through the peephole; there are two policemen waiting outside. *What the heck could they want?* I hand comb my hair and open the door.

"Ah, hello … can I help you?" I ask politely from behind the ajar door.

"Anouk Fowler?" one of the policemen asks in a serious tone.

Startled, I hesitate. "Yes."

"Good morning, Mrs. Fowler. I'm detective Kenneth Mantle, and this is Detective Stevens. We're from the Atlanta Police Department. I wonder if we could come inside and ask a few questions about the events of the evening of the fifteenth of June twenty-twelve."

"Err … yes … please come in," I say, directing them into the living room. "Please have a seat. Can I get either of you a cup of tea … coffee?" I stutter.

"No, thank you, ma'am," they reply in unison as they take a seat on the leather couch. I take a seat across from them. They look like polar opposites. Detective Mantle is brown-eyed, middle-aged, short, and thin. He has unruly salt and pepper, medium-length hair and thin, pursed lips. Conversely, Detective Stevens is a blue-eyed, baby-faced twenty-something. He's tall and plump, with a crewcut like a Marine. His hands are visibly shaking as he opens his notepad.

"So how can I help you?" I ask.

Detective Mantle is quick to respond. "Mrs. Fowler, the New York Police Department contacted us here in Atlanta requesting that we conduct further investigation into the events of the evening of June fifteenth this year. They sent over their police report, and there appear to be some unanswered questions," he says, frowning at the paperwork in his hand.

"Look … I'm sorry. I really can't help you. I don't remember anything about the accident," I say, shaking my head.

"Can you tell us what you do know?" he asks abruptly.

"All I can tell you is that I had a car accident. I can't recall any details."

"Can you tell us where you were driving to that evening?"

"I was driving home from work."

"I thought you couldn't remember, Mrs. Fowler," Detective Mantle prods as he jots something on his notepad.

"Well, err … my husband told me I was driving home. It was raining, and my car lost control; I hit a lamppost at high speed. That's all I know." I shrug.

Detective Mantle's eyes narrow, and he tilts his head to one side.

I can't help but feel he doesn't believe me. *I should call Jonathan.* "I think you should talk to my husband. He can give you more information," I say quietly.

"Oh, we will talk to your husband, Mrs. Fowler, in due course. But right now, we want to talk to you about what *you* know. What was your relationship to Miss Mia Richardson?"

"I don't know a Mia … Why?" I ask, shaking my head, confused.

Detective Mantle shoots a quick glance at Stevens and raises an eyebrow. "You don't know Mia Richardson?" Mantle asks, surprised. He sits forward in his seat.

"No. Look, Detective, I've told you what I know. I'm not sure if you're aware, but I have amnesia … retrograde amnesia. I don't have any memories of the accident or anything that happened before it," I stammer, shaking my head.

"I'm sorry to hear that, Mrs. Fowler. That must be very difficult for you," he states empathetically. "Are you able to form new memories?"

"Yes," I reply, now feeling somewhat defensive.

"Well, we do have a copy of the police report that indicates you were hospitalized for some time as a result of the accident. It says that because of the head injuries you sustained, NYPD was unable to interview you," he says, looking at the report in his hand.

"Detective Mantle, why now? I mean, it's been four months since the accident. Why are you asking me these questions now?" I ask with a hint of frustration.

"Mrs. Fowler, your doctors advised NYPD that they couldn't interview you because you weren't able to provide cogent responses, so the investigation went into their cold case files for a while, given your expected recovery period." After a brief pause, he adds matter-of-factly, "Your husband also used his legal muscle to defer questioning at the time."

"How do you mean?" I ask, surprised by this revelation.

"Well, Mrs. Fowler, in light of your public persona, your husband was concerned about attracting unwanted media attention," he says as he flicks through pages of the report.

"That doesn't surprise me. My husband has been protective, naturally. My neighbor, Brianna, and my husband have both mentioned that the accident was reported by the media, though."

Detective Mantle pulls a pair of reading glasses out of his shirt pocket and puts them on. "Ma'am, NYPD mentions here in the report that one media outlet did in fact air some news about it briefly, just prior to your husband threatening legal action. According to this, the only information released to the media was that you were involved in a car accident and were being treated in the hospital. No further details were released." He pauses for just a moment before continuing. "Mrs. Fowler, why did you and your husband move to Atlanta? You clearly have a successful business in New York." Detective Mantle eyes me sternly.

"My husband and I thought a fresh start away from the city would aid in my recuperation. My husband's parents live here in Atlanta, and my father-in-law has a law firm here. But he's been unwell and wants to retire, so my husband is taking over the firm. You know, keep it in the family ... Perhaps you can tell me what you know, Detective Mantle," I ask, now exasperated.

"Mrs. Fowler—"

"Anouk, please." I say it sweetly to hide the fact that I'm losing patience with his line of questioning.

"Anouk, were you aware that your car was following Mia Richardson's car on the night of June fifteenth twenty-twelve?"

"No, I wasn't aware—"

"And were you aware, ma'am, that your car hit Mia Richardson's car from behind and that the impact forced her car off the road into a lamppost, killing her instantly?"

What did he just say?! I pause momentarily, trying to process the information he has just delivered to me.

"Oh my god. No! No! I didn't know that at all," I say, grabbing my chest. I feel a tightness there, and I can't catch my breath. "What?! I killed someone? Is that what you're saying?" I gasp.

"Anouk ... Mrs. Fowler, are you OK?" Detective Mantle asks sincerely. He gets up and comes over to put one hand on my shoulder. He appears genuine in his concern.

He continues in a quiet, reassuring tone, "Anouk, we're still doing the accident investigation and piecing together exactly what happened that night. That's why we're here to talk with you. There's many unanswered questions, and we need to determine the order of events. But what we do know is that your car hit Miss Richardson's car."

"I didn't know I hit someone else's car or that someone was killed! I need to call Jonathan. Oh my god, why on earth wouldn't Jonathan have told me this?" I sob, rising from my seat.

"You mean your husband never told you? Didn't any family or friends?" Detective Mantle asks, his mouth gaping in shocked surprise.

"No. I'm not sure ... Maybe he did tell me about it, and I just forgot. I did have short-term memory problems early on after the accident," I ramble in my confusion. "I guess I never asked my husband. It's not like I would ask lots of questions about something I can't even remember," I say.

"I guess not," he replies softly.

I glance over at Detective Stevens. His smile has disappeared and been replaced by a sympathetic frown. He hasn't said a word but has been hastily taking notes.

"Anouk, would there be a reason, any reason at all that you may know of, why your husband could have, hypothetically speaking, of course, kept information about the details of the accident from you?" Mantle says sympathetically.

"No. But knowing my husband like I do, he probably didn't want to upset or traumatize me. It was a difficult time, you know, this year. My recovery was difficult, and it was very hard on my husband. I can't remember the accident, anyway, so he probably felt there was no need to mention it. He wanted me to focus on my recovery," I say, wiping the tears from my eyes with a tissue as I sit down again.

"What about friends or family? I find it odd, and don't you, too, that no one told you about the death of the other person involved in the accident or that it never came up in conversation," he says, looking at me quizzically.

He doesn't believe me. "Look, Detective, I have few friends, believe it or not. I don't have contact with my parents, and I'm an only child. Well, I do have one close friend. My work colleague, Tom. He was, or I mean he *is*, my best friend, or so I'm told. I have no memories of him, either. Jonathan can give you his contact number in New Y—"

"No need," Detective Mantle interrupts. "NYPD forwarded Tom's contact details to us. They spoke to him yesterday afternoon briefly. Tom is who gave them your address here."

"So what did Tom say?" I ask.

"NYPD said he had nothing to say other than that he knew of the accident. He said he hasn't seen you since."

I need to call Jonathan. "I don't want to sound rude, but I think I've answered enough questions for today, and I have some errands to run," I say, standing up and holding out my hand to shake theirs.

"Yes, of course. Thank you for your time, Anouk. We'll be in touch," Detective Mantle says as he and Detective Stevens start walking toward the front door.

"Here's my number. If you remember anything, anything at all, please give me a call, OK?" Detective Mantle says, turning to hand me his card.

"Detective, this Mia, the woman who was killed … did she have a family?" I ask.

Detective Mantle glances briefly at Detective Stevens. "She had a kid. Not married," Mantle replies matter-of-factly.

Detective Stevens nudges Detective Mantle and whispers something I can't hear.

"Look, Anouk, I'm sorry I'm the one to have to tell you this, but Detective Stevens and I think there's something you should know. Given that the investigation has been reopened, you're going to find out sooner or later, anyway. You knew Mia Richardson. In fact, you'd known her for many years," he says hesitantly in a soft voice.

"What? How did I know her?"

"Mia was your business partner."

* * *

CHAPTER SIX

MIA

February 1st, 1995
Morning

I wash my hands, staring at the spots that have appeared on my complexion in the restroom mirror. *Fucking acne*! I rummage through my handbag to find some makeup. I locate a mascara that is all but empty and a strawberry-flavored lip gloss. *That will have to do*. I apply a coat of lip gloss and a few coats of mascara in an attempt to illuminate my brown eyes. I look at my watch: It's 9:05 a.m. *Shit*! *I'm late*. I was supposed to be there five minutes ago.

I frantically push my long hair behind my ears and take off my winter jacket to tuck my shirt into my tight jeans. *Crap! I've put on more weight*. It's not going to make a good impression being late on my first day at design school. I scurry down the long corridor toward the classroom and knock on the door. I see through the window that the class is already seated. *Oh no.*

A middle-aged woman in a fuchsia pantsuit opens the door and greets me. "Good morning,"

"Hi. I'm Mia. Sorry I'm late," I say breathlessly, holding out my hand to shake hers.

She is immaculately groomed. Her gray-blonde hair is neatly pulled back into a loose bun. "I'm Miss Catherill. Come in and find a seat," she says in a welcoming voice.

Phew! She doesn't seem too bothered by my lateness. I look around the room. There must be at least twenty-five students. The class is predominately female, and there are only two open seats left. A pretty blonde girl in the back of the class flashes me an inviting smile, and I decide on the open seat next to hers.

"Mia, I was just saying to the class that I'm very excited to have all of you as my students this year. I want to congratulate each and every one of you on achieving your placement here at Catherill School of Design," she says, scanning the room.

Miss Catherill is considered one of *the* best teachers in fashion design. She is a successful fashion designer in her own right. This is the reason I am here: to learn from the best so that I can be the best.

"This year, you will be challenged, and I do expect you to be on time," Miss Catherill continues, giving me a quick glance as she says it.

Oh no. She was *bothered by my lateness.*

"Hi, I'm Anouk," a voice beside me whispers, distracting me from Miss Catherill's lecture. It's the pretty blonde. She's giving me a wave beneath the top of her desk, out of Miss Catherill's view.

"I'm Mia," I whisper quickly back at her, somewhat annoyed by her interruption of the lecture and now worried I might have missed something important.

Miss Catherill spends the morning sharing her personal success story and inviting random participants to come to the front of the class to share their achievements and career dreams of a future in fashion design.

Thankfully, Miss Catherill soon announces it's time for a break and saves me from the boredom of having to hear another person talk about how clever they are. What a bunch of suck-ups. I rise from my seat and follow the class toward the door.

"Hey, Mia, do you want to go to the cafeteria?" a friendly voice behind me asks.

I turn around. *It's the annoying blonde girl.* "Yeah. Why not," I concede, shrugging my shoulders. I'm not good at making conversation with strangers, but she seems friendly enough.

"It's Anouk, did you say?" I ask with reservation, hoping I've pronounced her name correctly as we walk out of the classroom.

"Yes," she says, nodding her head.

"I haven't heard that name before. It's different," I say politely, although I can't help but think it's a strange name.

"My dad named me after one of his favorite actresses," she discloses, flicking her fine blonde hair over her shoulder.

"So, where you from?" she asks without hesitation.

"Philadelphia. And you?"

"I live here in New York."

"With your folks?"

"No. I own an apartment opposite Central Park. I live by myself . . ."

Holy smoke! She owns an apartment? Probably born with a silver spoon in her mouth.

"Where are you staying?" she asks in a friendly voice.

"Oh … um … I'm lodging at a youth hostel until I can get my own place and find a part-time job," I reply.

We walk downstairs to the cafeteria, which is already alive with the sound of chatting students and the aroma of brewed coffee and fried food. We both order a hot chocolate. I manage to find a table for us among the sea of students. It's too cold to sit outside today, even though the winter sun is out, and the sky is clear. *I can't wait for winter to be over.*

"Where do your folks live?" I ask.

"Here in New York."

"So how come you don't live with them?" I ask.

"I just couldn't wait to move out and get my own place," she mutters.

"How did they feel about you moving out on your own?" I ask, taking a sip of my hot chocolate.

"They didn't like it, but I said, 'Daddy, if you don't buy me my own apartment in New York, I will never speak to you or Mom again.' I'm an only child, and my dad is a Wall Street stockbroker. He's loaded, so I knew they would do it—buy me an apartment," she sniggers. "I haven't spoken to them for a while now, though."

This girl really is a piece of work. "Why don't you speak to them? Were they not good parents?" I ask, confused. *At least you had parents, you spoiled brat!*

"In some ways, they were good parents; absent mostly. I was practically raised by nannies, mind you. I was their living doll they dressed up and played with once in a while when they weren't working, holiday-ing, or going to social events with the New York elite. They were also controlling, treating me like a twelve-year-old errant child. They think I'm too selfish," she scoffs.

No shit.

"So you want to be a fashion designer?" she asks, taking a sip of her hot chocolate.

She's staring at me with wide eyes. *No, I'm here to learn how to bake cakes, blondie.* She seems sincere enough, so I try to cut her some slack and answer her question as politely as I can.

"Yeah. I've always wanted to do fashion design since I was fairly young," I explain, taking another sip of my hot chocolate.

"Me too!" she exclaims, sounding like an excited little schoolgirl. There is something very innocent about her and a naïveté. "I want to own my own fashion label one day," she says confidently.

"What do you like to design?" I ask, trying to sound like I actually want to make conversation with her.

"I have no idea how to design ... yet," she laughs. "I just love fashion. I'm not naturally creative, so I'm here to learn," she says, placing a lone strand of hair behind her ear with a manicured finger.

"So, how did you get into Catherill School of Design?" I ask.

"I just applied and got in," she says matter-of-factly, shrugging her shoulders.

Fuck, she's conceited.

She continues "My dad makes considerable dona-tions to the design school every year, so they weren't going to say no to me unless they wanted to lose their funding," she scoffs, tilting her head to one side.

This girl is so arrogant. Everything about her oozes wealth—her pearl necklace, designer handbag, and her black designer suit. She is dressed like a woman twice her age, but her face suggests she must only be in her late teens. She really is pretty—heart-shaped face, full lips, blue eyes, and flawless pale skin. She has a perfect size four petite figure. I'd give anything to look like her.

"And you?" she asks, raising an eyebrow.

"I received a scholarship." *Yes, blondie. I got into design school on my talent, not via Daddy's wallet.*

"Scholarship? Congratulations!" she says in a loud voice.

"Thank you," I murmur, embarrassed that she has just announced it to the whole cafeteria.

"So, tell me, what do you like to design?" she asks, studying my face. Despite her arrogance, there is a subtle warmth about her.

"Evening dresses. My mother was a seamstress, and she would make the most amazing cocktail and evening dresses. My inspiration comes from her creations, from watching her when I was little."

"Does she still sew?"

"Both my parents died years ago … in a car accident when I was seven," I say quietly. A lump rises in my throat.

"I'm so sorry, Mia ... for your loss," she says. "So who raised you then?" she frowns.

Geez ... this girl asks a lot of questions. "Well, I was in and out of foster homes for a couple of years. A barren couple adopted me when I was nine," I say, stirring my hot chocolate. *Don't think about it, Mia.*

"Were they good to you ... your adoptive parents?" she asks.

"No, they weren't. I hate them, actually. I took a part-time job at sixteen and saved as much money as I could so I could come here to get away from them. I don't like to talk about it . . ." I shudder at just the thought.

"We'd better get back to class," Anouk says, rising from her seat. She turns to me. "You know, Mia, if you need somewhere to stay, you're welcome to stay with me," she says, touching me on my shoulder as we start walking back to class.

Holy smoke! I'm taken aback by her generosity, and I'm momentarily at a loss for words. "Anouk, that's a very generous offer. I couldn't ... I mean ... I can't pay you rent until I find a job," I stutter, reeling from her offer.

"Don't worry about that. I won't charge you rent, but we can split the other costs when you find a job, OK? It's up to you," she says matter-of-factly.

"Are you sure?" I ask.

She nods and gives me a reassuring smile.

Say yes, Mia. "OK. Thank you!" I blurt out in excitement.

"Good, then. It's a done deal," she says before she walks ahead of me back to class.

Why is she being kind to me? I've only just met her, and I have nothing to offer her. We don't have anything in common at all apart from a love of fashion and the fact that we both share a hatred for our parents. *Maybe that's it?* Perhaps she can see a little piece of herself in me. Maybe I've found a kindred spirit, one I'm bonded to by a common love and a common hate.

* * *

CHAPTER SEVEN

ANOUK

October 17th, 2012
Evening

It's 7:30 p.m., and Jonathan is still not home from work. I pace the house. *Where the heck is he?* He hasn't answered his cell phone all day. I put Charlie to bed, run a bath, and pour in some peppermint-scented body wash in the hopes that it will ease some of my anxiety. The meeting with Detectives Mantle and Stevens replayed in my head all afternoon as I frantically cleaned the house to take my mind off the news of Mia's death. I slide into the bath, lie back, and close my eyes. My thoughts turn to Mia Richardson, the poor woman I hit with my car. The woman who *I* may have killed. I feel guilt and anguish, not knowing what happened or what I did.

Oh my god … Did I kill her? Am I responsible for taking away a child's mother? Why did my car hit hers? Who was she? Were we close friends? I ask these questions over and over again. *And why didn't Jonathan tell me about her? For heaven's sake, if she was my business partner, why did he keep this information from me?*

"There you are," Jonathan's voice startles me into an upright position, and I splash water and bubbles onto the bathroom floor. He's standing in the doorway with a seductive grin, his tie undone. He has a bottle of wine in one hand and two wine glasses in the other.

"Can I join you?" he asks suggestively.

"Where the heck have you been?" I snap.

"At work. I told you this morning I'd be working late tonight. Did you forget?" he asks, walking toward me.

He takes a seat at the end of the bathtub and pours a glass of wine that he passes to me.

"I've been trying to call you all afternoon. Why didn't you return my calls?" I grouse, snatching the glass from him.

"I was in court all day with Dad downtown. I had to turn my phone off, sweetheart," he says calmly.

"I had the Atlanta police here today."

He abruptly stops pouring wine into his glass. But then he continues, sounding unperturbed despite his surprised stopping of movement. "What did they want?" he asks.

"What do you think, Jonathan? Is there something you should have told me?" I ask testily. I feel a sob rising in my throat. *Don't cry, Anouk.*

"I don't—"

"Don't bullshit me, Jonathan. I'm in no mood tonight!" I interrupt, slapping the surface of the bath with my hand and startling him. "Why didn't you tell me about Mia? Mia Richardson … you know, the woman who died," I sneer.

His mouth drops open, and he appears startled by this announcement.

"I had my reasons," he says apprehensively.

"What reasons? They'd better be good," I say, taking a gulp of wine.

"The reason is simply that I didn't want to upset you," he says, running his fingers through his hair in frustration.

"You lied to me!"

"It's the truth, Anouk," he sighs. "Just think about it. How would it have helped your recovery knowing about Mia's death? In the weeks following the accident, you still appeared to have no memory of the accident or of Mia, so I just didn't mention it to you, OK?" he says, exasperated. "I just wanted you to focus on getting well, so I told you that you were driving home from work when your car hit a lamppost. I didn't want you blaming yourself for her death. I was going to tell you the truth about Mia's death when the time was right," he says, leaning over to stroke my bubble-covered leg.

"The police told me she was my business partner, Jonathan. You could have told me that! How do you think I feel finding out this information from other people? You should have told me this!"

"What exactly did the police say?" he asks with a frown.

"They wanted to know what I knew about that night. They've reopened the investigation into the accident."

"What did you tell them?" he asks coolly, taking a sip of wine.

"I told them I have no memory of the accident and that they should talk to you. Why was I following Mia that night?" I ask.

"I don't know. Maybe we'll know the answer to that question when you get your memory back."

I put my wine down. "Oh my god. What if *I* killed her?" I say, holding my head in my hands in anguish.

"It was an accident. It wasn't your fault, OK?" he says in a reassuring tone.

"How do you know?" I ask.

"Look, the police in New York weren't sure how it happened at the time, either. All we know is that you hit her car, and her car hit a lamppost. What I don't know is why you were following her that night. You'd told me that day that you were heading straight home after work," he says, taking another sip of his wine.

"What was she like? Tell me all about her," I ask.

"Mia was … talented. You met her in your late teens at the Catherill School of Design in New York. She had a rough childhood; she was orphaned and then adopted. You took pity on her and let her stay with you . . ." He pauses reflectively, then continues, "You were roommates for years. You had the business brains, the drive, and the determination, and she had a natural creative flair for fashion design. You were determined to own your own fashion label, and she was determined to be famous for her designs. You two had always planned to work together. So when you started Designite Fashion House, she worked for you as a designer, and you eventually made her a partner when she threatened to leave the business unless you did so."

"What did she look like?" I ask.

"I can show you a picture of her if you like," he says with a half-smile, raising his eyebrows.

"Yes, please do." I nod to him, taking another sip of wine.

He leaves the room and returns about five minutes later, carrying a photo album. It's the same one I'd seen when I was unpacking in Jonathan's library.

"This is Mia," he says, pointing at a photo.

It's the picture of me, Jonathan, and Tom at a fashion show with the stunningly glamorous long-haired, tall, and leggy brunette.

"I saw this photo when I was unpacking. I thought that was a photo of one of the fashion house models," I say, pointing at the photo.

"Yes, she could pass as a model there," he says.

"Did she have a partner?"

"I don't know. I never met one." He shrugs. "You once told me that she had a crush on Tom."

"She had a child. What if I'm responsible for taking a mother away from her child?" I stutter, gulping the last drop of my wine and shaking my head in frustrated confusion.

"Now, now. You can't go blaming yourself, OK? I'll talk to the police," he says.

"I don't know what or who to believe anymore, Jonathan … By the way, the police also said that you used your legal muscle to stop information about my accident from getting out to the media. Why didn't you tell me this?" I ask, reaching my wine glass out to him and gesturing for him to top it up.

He sighs as he pours me another glass of wine. "I was protecting your brand, of course. You know that I have your best interests at heart. You're well known, and like I've said before, you're a private person with a public persona. I didn't want the media hounding you. You were in grave condition, Anouk, and at the time, the doctors told me that you might end up in a vegetative state. You were in a coma, and I didn't want that being reported in the media. And neither would you! Besides, I didn't know at that point if my wife was going to live or die. You can't imagine the situation I was in. I didn't want photographers at my door while I was grieving. The business always came first, so I thought I was doing what you would have wanted me to do, OK? You weren't able to make those decisions, so I had to. For heaven's sake, Anouk, this has been hard on me, too!" he says, gulping the last of his wine and clanking his wine glass down hard on the bathroom counter.

He slides his tie off from under his collar in frustration and storms out of the bathroom without saying a word.

Darn! I get out of the bath and put on a robe before following him. He's not in the bedroom. I walk downstairs and go to the living room, where I find him sitting in the dark, staring forlornly at the fireplace.

"I'm sorry," I say, kneeling at his feet beside him. "I know you have my best interests at heart. I know you were protecting me," I slur, now feeling the full effects of the wine.

"I'm sorry, too," he says, pulling me up onto his lap and cradling me in his arms like a child.

* * *

CHAPTER EIGHT
ANOUK

October 19th, 2012
Morning

I check my cell phone for text messages from Jonathan as I ride in the cab on my way to Emory. It's been a while since Jonathan has had to care for Charlie on his own, without my help, so I'm feeling somewhat anxious. Conversely, Jonathan had appeared ecstatic this morning about spending time alone with Charlie, so I'm comforted by the knowledge that he'll be attentive and will no doubt spoil our son. I put my cell phone away and relax in the back seat; I'm content with catching a cab for now. Ironically, driving is one of the few things that I can still remember how to do, but I don't have the confidence to drive alone just yet. The Volvo was a practical purchase just before we moved to Atlanta. Jonathan had to hand back his company car, and the two thousand and seven red Chevy Corvette C6 convertible he'd bought me for my thirtieth birthday was, of course, a total write-off, broken beyond repair. Jonathan test drove a number of vehicles for us to consider, and we eventually settled on the Volvo after I took it for a test drive with his guidance. Jonathan thought it would be a safe family car, although I know he misses the Corvette. Being a car enthusiast, he told me that he cherished the C6. And although it was my car, he relished the times he got to drive it on scenic byways during our weekend getaways to New Paltz. I often joke with Jonathan that he should have been a mechanic rather than a lawyer. He is always going on about some model or another and their mechanics.

The cab pulls up outside Emory Hospital, and I step out and walk in the busy entrance. I'm overcome by the all-too-familiar smell of the hospital, a mingling of disinfectant, antiseptic, and bleach. Its sterile scent reminds me of the countless days I spent in one back in New York. It makes me feel more anxious.

"Hello, can I help you?" a gray-haired lady calls out to me as I approach the hospital reception desk.

"I'm Anouk Fowler ... I'm here to start ... my outpatient rehab program today," I stutter.

"Welcome, Anouk. Let me check who will be seeing you today," she says, tapping on her computer keyboard. "Annette McDonald, our occupational therapist, will be seeing you first," she says, looking over her black-rimmed glasses. "Can you fill in these forms please while you are waiting?" she asks, handing me a clipboard and pen.

Darn. "I can't read very well," I whisper.

"Annette will help you. Please take a seat over there," she says softly, pointing to the area full of waiting patients.

I take a seat next to a middle-aged man in a wheelchair. He looks rather forlorn, slumped in his wheelchair, expressionless, his vacant eyes staring blankly into the distance. The right side of his head is partially shaved, exposing a long thick scar. The stitches are still visible and tinged with dried blood. I try not to stare, but I can't help but take an occasional look. His scar reminds me of the photos that Jonathan showed me of my head injuries after the accident.

Ugh! I get an ill feeling in the pit of my stomach, and I shudder at the thought of those early days following the accident—the intense pain, the confusion, the isolation, and the feeling of hopelessness. I can't help but wonder whether this man has suffered a similar fate.

"Anouk Fowler?" a brown-haired lady calls to the waiting area.

"Here," I mouth, holding my hand up.

"Hello, Anouk," the brown-haired lady greets me. "I'm Annette McDonald. I'll be your occupational therapist throughout your rehabilitation program with us. Let's go into my office," she says, indicating that I should follow her.

"Please take a seat," she says, putting her long hair up into a ponytail before she opens a file on her desk.

"So, Anouk, I've read through your medical records from Mount Sinai. I'm sincerely sorry to hear what happened to you," she says in a sympathetic voice. "Tell me, how are you doing at the moment?"

"I'm doing OK. I feel myself getting stronger. I do get tired in the afternoon."

"That's to be expected, Anouk, given the type of brain injury you sustained. The tiredness should improve over time, though," she says as she flicks through my medical records. "Your medical records state here that you were diagnosed with an extreme form of retrograde amnesia and that you have no memory of who you are or events that occurred prior to the trauma. Tell me, how are you doing with day-to-day tasks at home?" she asks with a questioning look.

"I know instinctively how to do certain things, like, for example, getting dressed in the morning, how to apply my makeup, how to clean my house, how to use the toaster." *How to have sex. Don't say it out loud, Anouk.* "I can remember most words, names for colors and objects. I know these things. Why is that, Annette? Why is it I can't remember who I am, I can't remember my past, but I can remember how to use the damned toaster?" I ask in exasperation.

"With the type of brain injuries you sustained, episodic memory is typically more severely affected than semantic memory. That's why you can still remember words, how everyday objects work, and general knowledge like colors but don't remember experiences or specific events in your life. From what you've told me, your procedural memory appears relatively unaffected. For example, your memory of skills, habits, and how to perform everyday functions. And that is why you can still remember how to use the toaster." She continues, glancing at my medical records as she speaks. "It says here that you also had some physical challenges with the use of your limbs on your right side and have had trouble with your speech. Is that correct?" she asks with a raised eyebrow.

"Yes, although I do feel the strength on my right side is improving. I use a walking stick sometimes. I still have trouble finding the right words. I can think the words I want to say, but sometimes I can't articulate them out loud," I explain.

"Your speech this morning is very good." She smiles. "Your speech will usually be at its best in the morning, after you're well rested. My experience is that patients with similar head injuries regain the strength in their limbs with physical therapy. Your speech may also improve with therapy. However, some patients have been left with permanent damage. It's hard to say in your case. Only time will tell. It's important, though, that you keep to your rehab schedule and attend two days per week here, OK?" she says, leaning forward in her chair. Her brown eyes study mine.

"I keep having the same horrible dream over and over again. It's vague, but I'm sure they're memories of the car accident," I say hesitantly.

"That's not uncommon in patients who've suffered a head injury. In some cases, memories of trauma manifest themselves unconsciously in the form of dreams," she says, taking notes as she speaks. "Have you had any other symptoms or challenges since the head injury?" she asks cocking her head to one side.

"Um ... I can't read or write very well."

"I can put together a tailored program to help you learn to read and write again," she says in an upbeat voice. "Have you had any flashbacks, like déjà vu, or have you been able to recall *any* events or experiences that occurred prior to the trauma?"

"Yes!" I exclaim. "My husband and I have only just moved here from New York, and when I was unpacking boxes, I found a used pregnancy test. When I saw it, I got a flashback, a memory, I think. I remembered the time I showed my husband the positive result."

"Good. That's reassuring. Can you remember anything from your childhood?" she asks.

"There's a swing under an oak tree in our backyard here, and when I first saw it, I had déjà vu or a sense that it was like one I had in my backyard when I was little. I'm not too sure," I say, shaking my head.

"Good. The fact that you can recall these memories recently is very positive indeed. How is your short-term memory at the moment?" she asks, looking at her notes.

"My short-term memory has improved over the past couple of months. My husband has noticed it too."

"Hmm," she says, looking reflective. "You could start doing some mind exercises that will also help. I can give you some—"

"Will I ever get my long-term memory back?" I interrupt.

"It's hard to say." She sighs, puts down her pen, and leans back in her chair before continuing. "Yours is an extreme case. And every case is different. For experiences and events that occurred nearest in time to the car accident, those memories may never be recovered. This is because the neural pathways of newer memories are not as strong as older ones that have been strengthened by years of retrieval. That is possibly why you can remember the swing from your early childhood, but you can't remember other experiences or events just prior to the accident."

She picks up my medical records from her desk and flicks through, biting her bottom lip in concentration. "What did you do for an occupation?" she asks as she scans the records.

"I was a fashion designer … apparently," I quip. It sounds so ridiculous every time I say it out loud.

"Have you tried to design or draw since the accident?"

"No, I haven't. Will I ever remember who I am?" I ask, feeling a sob rise in my throat.

"While there is no cure for retrograde amnesia, it's important that you start jogging your memory. By this, I mean that, if you feel up to it, you must try to get back into the routine you had prior to the car accident. You should try to start drawing again, Anouk, or take time to look over your designs. Better still, go back to work. Catch up with the people you used to spend time with, do hobbies that you used to do, visit places you used to go with your husband. Doing things that you experienced in the past may help you to remember."

As much as try to hold it together, I start to cry. "How can I? I don't remember what I used to do or who I used to speak to. I don't know who I am."

Annette pulls a tissue from the box on her desk and passes it to me. "I understand. It must be so frustrating and frightening for you. I can't imagine what it must be like for you right now. I can give you some hope though. I did have a patient once who had a similar situation to yours. He regained his long-term memory. He got back into his old routine, caught up with the people he used to be friends with, and went back to his job. It gradually came back to him. Maybe there's hope for you too. Don't give up, Anouk. I'll help you," she says in a soft voice, placing a reassuring hand on mine.

* * *

CHAPTER NINE
ANOUK

October 20th, 2012
Morning

I didn't sleep much last night. I kept thinking about Mia, and after Jonathan went to bed, I did an internet search and stumbled across quite a few of her social media profile photos. They were mainly selfies she had taken during her overseas travels and various outdoor recreational activities in recent years. She seemed to keep herself fit. It was when I came across a much older photo of the two of us together that I became emotional. It was taken outside the doors of the Catherill School of Design. We were young, and our long hair was down.

I recognized the much younger version of myself right away. Apart from the visible signs of aging, I haven't changed that much over the years. Mia, however, was more round-faced and fuller-figured in her youth. We were posing side-by-side, our hands raised above our heads, high up in the air, and we were smiling joyfully. We appeared full of life. I stared at that photo for a very long time, studying Mia's happy face, all the while wondering what she was like and what we were like together.

Last night, I felt a depth of sadness that I haven't felt or allowed myself to feel in a while. I mourned for Mia, the loss of our friendship, and mostly for the loss of my history, the lost memory of who I once was.

I reflected on Annette's advice to get back into my old routine, as I have so many questions that I want to ask Tom in person, but I'm not ready to go back to New York and leave Charlie.

I arrive at Brianna's house the next morning with a homemade tea cake in hand.

"Anouk, I'm so pleased you came." Brianna greets us at her door in a red suit and kisses me on each cheek. I now feel underdressed in my white jeans, khaki shirt, and tan wedges.

"Hello, Charlie." She waves at him.

Maybe she does like kids? "Morning, Brianna. I made an orange tea cake," I lie. Actually, it was

Jonathan who ended up making it because I couldn't read the instructions for the recipe, something the rehabilitation program at Emory can help with, no doubt.

"Oh, honey, you shouldn't have," she says, taking it from me. "It smells delicious. Thank you. Please come in," she says, waving her hand to usher us inside impatiently.

I leave the stroller at the front door and carry Charlie in toward the sound of women chattering.

"The ladies are here, and they can't wait to meet *you*," Brianna says in her southern drawl.

Shit! She's told them who I am.

The house smells of freshly baked sweets, brewed coffee, and women's perfume. I walk into her living room, trying my best to hide my limp. The home has a similar layout to mine; however, her interior design is French provincial, with antique furniture, chandeliers, vintage soft furnishings, and tasseled drapes. The house is spotless.

I am met by three well-dressed ladies of different ages sitting and drinking coffee. One of the younger women has a little girl on her lap.

"Ladies, I would like to introduce you to my new neighbor, Anouk Fowler. She just moved in a few doors down," Brianna announces theatrically.

"Hello, Anouk," they each reply in welcoming voices and with inviting smiles.

"Anouk, I'd like you to meet Leanne, Louise, and Kathy," Brianna says, pointing to each of them as she says their names.

Find your words, Anouk. "Hello. Nice to meet you all ... this is Charlie," I announce as I stroke Charlie's cheek with the back of my finger.

They have suddenly gone quiet and all look at me eagerly, like they are waiting for me to say something else.

Thankfully, Brianna continues. "And ladies, Anouk also just happens to be *the best* fashion designer in the United States!" she declares, clapping her hands in her animated fashion. She waves her hands up and down the sides of her body and nods to indicate that she is wearing one of my designs. The ladies start to clap.

Oh my god. I smile politely at each of them, trying to hide my rising embarrassment.

"Anouk, please take a seat," the auburn-haired lady with the little girl on her lap says, indicating for me to sit next to her. "I'm Leanne, and this is Emily."

"Hi. How old is Emily?" I ask, placing Charlie on my lap.

"She's just turned three. How old is Charlie?"

"He's nine months."

"You must be very busy, Anouk, traveling to and from New York and juggling a baby," she says, bouncing Emily on her lap.

How does she know I'm from New York? Brianna must have told her.

"Well, not really … It's a long story, but I'm not working at the moment. A friend of mine is running the business for me back in New York. I'm hoping to go back next year when Charlie is a little older," I explain. I don't want to discuss the accident with everyone today.

"I have a confession. I'm a huge fan of your clothing label. I bought an evening dress from one of your stores last year," she says shyly. "It's a shame you don't sell clothing for children," she adds.

Hmm. What a great idea. "That's not a bad idea, Leanne. I might look into doing that … in the future; thanks." I'll have to talk to Tom about the possibility of a clothing line for children. It's something I could potentially design, and Charlie would be my inspiration.

"Ladies, I've set up morning tea on the table outside in the garden," Brianna says to us as she carries two plates of fancily decorated cupcakes. "Please help yourselves. The little ones can play in the sunshine."

Outside, I follow Charlie as he crawls on the grass, playing with the autumn leaves. Emily toddles next to him with her brown curls bouncing. Brianna and Leanne are deep in conversation, sharing their homemade recipes with each other next to the array of baked treats and coffee on the outside table. The other, seemingly older, women of the group, Louise and Kathy, are standing next to them, whispering to one another out of my earshot and giving me an occasional unnerving stare. Kathy in particular hasn't taken her eyes off me since I arrived.

"So, Anouk, tell me, what does your husband do?" Leanne asks when she walks over to stand beside me.

"He's a lawyer."

"Oh, really?" she muses. "Brianna and her husband, Eric, are lawyers too," she says before taking a bite of her cupcake.

More lawyers.

"Really? So ... err ... what do you do, Leanne?" I stutter. *Darn. Get your words out, Anouk*!

"I'm a stay-at-home mom. Sometimes I work in my husband Tony's business, you know, doing some of the administrative duties. He has a car dealership in town," she says.

I nod at her as I chew my last mouthful of one of Brianna's delicious cupcakes.

"Are you going to have another one?" Leanne asks.

"Another cupcake?" I ask.

"No," she giggles, placing a hand up to her mouth. "Another baby," she clarifies.

I smile and reply, "Oh ... um ... one is enough ... for now, at least. You?" I ask.

"I'm trying for another, but it's not happening. I would love for Emily to have a brother or sister." She sighs and then continues. "But I should be grateful; I have a beautiful, healthy child already. I know Brianna would give anything to have just one," she says with a hint of sadness in her brown eyes, looking over at Emily.

"Oh, I didn't—"

Brianna appears seemingly from nowhere and abruptly interrupts. "So, girls, what are you talkin' about?" she asks in her over-the-top Brianna way, putting her arms around our shoulders.

Leanne's face flushes. "Err … I was just telling Anouk that I'm trying for another baby," Leanne says to Brianna with a sheepish look.

"Ah, the joys of trying for offspring," Brianna laughs, taking a sip of her coffee as she looks over at Charlie and Emily playing on the grass. I'm not sure if she is being sarcastic. "I would love a little one, too, but you know, my eggs are all dried up," she says to me matter-of-factly in her southern drawl.

"Yep, that ship has sailed for me … my own fault though," she continues. Her blue eyes now look glassy.

"Why would it be your fault?" I ask, confused.

"Oh, honey, I put my career first and waited too long. I'm forty-two now."

What? She doesn't look forty-two at all. She could easily pass as a thirty-five-year-old.

She continues. "Leanne already knows this story. I tried IVF many times. I'm done with all that now. Eric, my husband, and I have accepted that it's not going to happen for us," she says taking another sip of her coffee.

"I'm so sorry, Brianna," I say, giving her a sympathetic frown.

"Now, now," she grouses, waving a finger at me. "I didn't invite you over for morning tea to talk about my fertility—or lack thereof," she laughs, placing my arm in hers and walking me away from Leanne.

"Anouk, speaking of children, each year, I organize the annual Children's Charity Ball in Atlanta in late June. It's considered one of *the* best balls in the state. The mayor always attends too. All funds raised go to children who are terminally ill. All the ladies here today are on the ball committee. Would you like to join? No pressure, of course, honey, but it's a lot of fun, *and* we would love your company," she says, giving me a warm smile.

"Of course. I'd like to help," I reply. "Brianna, Leanne mentioned that you and your husband are lawyers. My husband, Jonathan, is a lawyer too. He's just started at Ewan Fowler and Associates."

"Really? What a small world," she says, surprised. "I know Ewan well. He's somewhat of an icon here in Atlanta," she adds, but then she is quick to change the subject. "Now, Anouk, I need to ask you something, and again, I don't want you to feel pressured. I would absolutely love you forever if you could design a dress for me to wear to the charity ball next year. I'll pay you, of course. Puhleeze? For your biggest fan?" she asks, fluttering her eyelashes and giving me puppy dog eyes.

She really is overdramatic; she'd make a great actress. I can't help but find her amusing, and I laugh at her theatrical display.

"I'm very flattered, but I couldn't … I mean … I can't design right now," I whisper to her so the other ladies can't hear.

"Why are we whispering?" she whispers to me, her eyes wide.

"Because I don't really want the world to know that I can't design. I can't remember how to design, Brianna. Jonathan doesn't think it would be good publicity for Designite Fashion House if my memory loss gets out to the media … you know … impact on our brand," I whisper.

I await her reaction. Her demeanor is composed and calm. Surprisingly, she appears unfazed by the announcement that I can't remember how to design.

"Honey, I haven't and won't say a word to anyone about your memory loss. My lips are sealed," she says quietly, placing her hand over her mouth and pretending to zip her lips. "But it could be good practice for you, Anouk. You know, to get back in the saddle, so to speak. I don't need the dress until June. That should give you plenty of time," she says in a reassuring voice.

Geez, she's pushy. "I don't know. Let me think about it, OK?" I ask, trying to look over her shoulder to see where Charlie has gotten to in the yard. I can't see him.

"Brianna, have you seen Charlie?" I ask calmly, trying to contain the rising inner panic.

"I saw him on the grass with Emily a few minutes ago, honey. He's fine," she says, waving her hand dismissively.

Nonetheless, I go look around the garden and still don't see him. "Leanne, have you ... have you seen Charlie?" I ask, frantic and breathless.

"He's with Emily behind the oak tree, just over there," she says, pointing. I walk briskly over to the tree, doing my best to ensure my limp isn't too obvious.

"Emily!" Leanne calls, as she follows me.

I can hear Charlie babbling and Emily talking to him in a little voice. *Phew!* I get behind the tree. *Oh my god.* Charlie is holding hands with Emily, and he's standing, if only for a second or two at a time.

"Leanne ... he's walking!" I exclaim, holding my hands up to my face in disbelief.

"Emily, let go of Charlie's hand. Let's see if baby Charlie can walk on his own," Leanne says, stroking Emily's forehead.

The little girl's chubby hand lets go of his, and Charlie takes a step before falling down on the grass. Just then, Brianna comes over to see what all the commotion is about.

"Brianna, Charlie took his first steps," I boast.

"Well, honey, I think your son is destined for greatness," she says dryly in her southern drawl, patting my arm.

Louise and Kathy appear disinterested, continuing to occasionally whisper something to one another as they watch me watch Charlie. I'm now feeling uncomfortable and want to go home.

"Brianna, it's time for me to take Charlie home for his nap. I must go … It was nice to meet you all," I say to the other ladies.

Louise and Kathy briefly stop talking to one another to give me a polite wave of their hands.

"Anouk, what are you doin' on Thanksgiving?" Brianna asks.

"Nothing yet. Why?" I ask, bouncing Charlie on my hip.

"Leanne and Tony are comin' over to our place for Thanksgiving lunch. Why don't you and your husband join us too? Bring Charlie."

"It would be great for the husbands to get to-gether," Leanne chimes in. "Emily and Charlie can play together."

"OK. I'll talk to Jonathan. Goodbye, Leanne. I really must get going. Brianna, thank you for your hospitality."

"You're welcome. I'll walk you out," Brianna says, moving toward her front door. "Hon, I know we just met, but I feel like I've known you for years," she says with a broad smile.

Her comment takes me by surprise, but there's something genuine about Brianna. I trust her, and I too feel like I've known her for years.

"Me too," I nod.

She gives me a firm kiss on my cheek, and I leave Brianna's house content and with a sense that this could be the beginning of a long-term friendship.

* * *

CHAPTER TEN

ANOUK

October 20th, 2012
Evening

Jacques, the French chef, makes a grand entrance trailed by his assistant Michael, and they proceed to hastily take over my kitchen. They bring in trolleys of cookware, utensils, boxes of fresh produce, and of course two large white containers marked "Live Lobster." I can't help but feel a little squeamish thinking about the lobsters' soon-to-be fate as dinner on our plates.

Jacques is a middle-aged man with brown hair and wild, dark eyes. He is loud and animated with his hands. Michael, however, is a young, unassuming, blue-eyed blond. He scurries around the kitchen, jumping into action in response to bossy commands from Jacques.

I set the dinner table while Jonathan takes a shower.

"Madam, tonight, we are serving Nova Scotia lobster with butter, crispy potatoes, asparagus, and lemon wedges," Jacques informs me with a French accent that sounds a bit exaggerated to me. I wonder if he really *is* French.

"Can't wait," I respond with a hint of sarcasm.

"For dessert, we have a chocolate mascarpone mousse served with fresh strawberries and cream," he continues.

I can't believe the grand display we're putting on tonight for Jonathan's parents; I hope they are pleasant.

Jonathan arrives in the kitchen smelling of body wash and dressed in his favorite white shirt and chino pants. He scoops up Charlie, who is also well dressed for the occasion.

"Do I look OK?" I ask Jonathan, adjusting my dress.

"You look lovely. Doesn't Mommy look lovely, Charlie?" he coos at Charlie, nodding his head.

"Thanks," I say, finger combing my hair. I'm pleased that I decided to wear a simple black A-line dress with matching black closed-toe pumps.

Jonathan gets the chilled bottle of French champagne out of the fridge and puts it into a silver ice bucket on the table.

"Jonathan, put on some music. What do your folks like to listen to?" I ask.

"Dad likes classic jazz. I'll put on some Louis Armstrong," he says, passing Charlie to me as he goes over to the laptop on the kitchen counter.

Charlie starts to cry and wriggle in my arms, and the wafting smell of his dirty diaper hits me in the face. *Darn.*

"Jonathan, I'm taking Charlie upstairs to change him."

The front doorbell chimes just as I get to the top of the stairs. *Shit!* I quickly change Charlie and carry him slowly back down the stairs in a rather ungracious manner, trying my best not to limp. *Damn these stairs.* I curse myself for deciding to wear heels. Claire and Ewan are already standing at the bottom of the staircase talking with Jonathan. I don't remember their faces. They stop talking when they see me, and they don't return my smile; their eyes are firmly fixed on Charlie, wide with anticipation.

"Oh my god, Ewan, he's just like Jonathan at that age," Claire declares, fluttering her fake lashes. She's dressed in a blue suit, and she's wearing bold, gold earrings.

"Anouk, it's so good to see you again," she says, coming up to greet me with a kiss on my cheek; but she doesn't take her eyes off Charlie.

"Hello, Claire," I say in a welcoming voice, pretending I actually remember her.

"Anouk," Ewan says, giving me a warm smile as he picks up my right hand to kiss the back of it. He is good-looking for a man in his late sixties, distinguished, with slicked back gray wavy hair. He's dressed in a tailored black suit.

"Hi, Ewan; this is Charlie," I announce. They both swarm around Charlie, touching his hands as I hold him on my hip. Charlie gives them a cheeky smile and buries his head in my neck.

"Oh, he's so cute, Jonathan," Claire declares, giving a wave to Charlie.

Jonathan's eyes sparkle with pride. Charlie looks at Claire out of the corner of his eyes, his head still buried in my neck. I'm not surprised by his reaction; Charlie isn't used to strangers. She holds her hands out to Charlie, indicating that she's eager to hold him in her arms, but he isn't as keen, and he keeps his head firmly buried in my neck. Claire appears forlorn by his reaction to her, so I try to make polite conversation.

"Maybe you can hold Charlie later, Claire, once he becomes a little more familiar with you," I say, trying to excuse his reaction.

I can sense Claire's tension, and I too am starting to feel uncomfortable about the awkward situation we find ourselves in tonight.

Thankfully, Jonathan interrupts. "Mom, Dad, please come in and take a seat," he says as he ushers them into the formal dining room and pulls out their chairs to seat them at the dining table before placing Charlie in his high chair.

"Something smells good, son," Ewan says, looking through the doorway into the kitchen at Jacques and Michael.

"We're serving your favorite tonight, Dad ... Nova Scotia lobster."

"Jonathan, how lovely. You remembered," Claire chirps, looking over at Ewan.

"Thank you, son," Ewan smiles broadly, placing a hand on Jonathan's shoulder. His hazel eyes well up as he looks at Jonathan.

Charlie is playing with his bottle in his high chair, and Claire can't take her eyes off him. "Charlie is so much like Jonathan at that age," she says, placing a lone strand of her bobbed blonde hair behind her ear.

"Yes, he is, and he's a good-looking boy at that. He certainly has the Fowler genes!" Ewan says with a hearty chuckle.

"Ewan and I were sorry to hear about what happened to you. Are you OK?" Claire asks me in a concerned voice.

"Thank you, Claire. I'm doing OK, actually," I reply.

"Anouk is making a good physical recovery, Mom. She still hasn't gotten her memories back though.

Hopefully, they'll come back soon," Jonathan says, giving me a sympathetic look.

"I'm so sorry, Anouk," Claire says, patting my hand.

"Don't be. I'm thankful to be alive to watch Charlie grow up. Ewan, how are you doing after your surgery?" I ask in an attempt to direct the conversation away from me.

"Well, it's going to take a lot more than a coronary bypass operation to keep me down, although I'm taking things slower now. It's time to hand the reins of the business over to my son," he says, patting Jonathan on the arm.

Jacques arrives at the table to pour the champagne. "Sir, dinner is ready," Jacques says, almost losing his white chef's hat as he leans down to whisper in Jonathan's ear.

Jonathan nods at him and waves his hand, indicating that we are ready to be served our meal.

"Dinner is served," Jacques announces in a loud voice and bows to us dramatically. Michael appears out of the kitchen to serve plates that are laden with lobster.

"Michael, Charlie will just have some of the potatoes and asparagus, cut up, please. He won't have the lobster," I say politely, shaking my head. I am not going to serve a nine-month-old lobster. Besides, I don't want to risk Charlie having an allergic reaction to seafood at his age.

"More lobster for you, Ewan," I add with a smirk.

Ewan gives me a smile and a wink. I can see now where Jonathan gets his charisma. Ewan really is quite charming.

"Please start, everyone," Jonathan says.

"Anouk, I'm so pleased you decided to have children. Charlie is just adorable," Claire says matter-of-factly.

Her comment takes me by complete surprise, and I nearly choke on my champagne. Jonathan glares at me from across the table, communicating that he's worried about how I will respond to her.

"Yes. I am too, Claire. Charlie is a blessing," I say as I clear my throat and glare at Jonathan in the hope that he'll save me from having this conversation with her.

"You know, Anouk, when Jonathan told us after you got married that you never wanted children, I was heartbroken. I thought I would never be a grand-mother. I'm so thrilled you changed your mind. I'm so happy," she says, smiling at me with tears welling up in her blue eyes. "I'm just so sad that I've missed out on his first nine months."

Awkward.

"I'm sorry, Mom," Jonathan interrupts, stroking the back of her manicured hand from across the table. "Look, we're here in Atlanta now. Anouk and I want you and Dad to be a part of Charlie's life," Jonathan says to her reassuringly.

Claire nods as she carefully wipes her mascara-soaked tears away with a tissue.

"Son, I love the house. You will have to take us for a tour after dinner," Ewan says cheerfully through a mouthful of lobster. He appears unperturbed by Claire's emotional outburst, or he too is trying to redirect the conversation.

It's not long before Charlie starts to grizzle, arching his back as he pulls at the straps of his high chair.

"Jonathan, Charlie is getting tired. He needs to go to bed," I say.

Jonathan nods in agreement as he wipes his mouth with his napkin.

Claire offers shyly, "Anouk, I can put Charlie to bed for you. That is, of course, if it's OK with you and Jonathan." Claire looks at Jonathan to seek his approval, and Jonathan gives me a reassuring nod.

"OK, Claire … If you don't mind … he may be difficult to settle," I stutter. I really don't like the idea of Claire putting Charlie to bed at all. I'm worried about how Charlie will react to being alone with *her*. But Claire appears excited by the prospect, so I concede.

"Charlie's room is on the left when you reach the top of the stairs. His pajamas and a fresh diaper are already on his changing table," I say, trying to sound like I'm actually OK with her offer. Internally, I'm battling with my motherly instincts, like an overprotective bear wanting to protect her cub from an intruding stranger.

"Oh, thank you," Claire says as she rises from her seat and proceeds to lift Charlie out of his high chair. Surprisingly, he is unfazed by her picking him up. Perhaps he can sense that she's family, and he's calm as she holds him in her arms and kisses him on the cheek.

"Come on, Charlie; let Grandma put you to bed," she says.

He gives her a smile as she carries him upstairs, cooing softly in his ear. I relax briefly with the knowledge that he is calm in her arms. Ewan immediately turns to Jonathan and starts talking business as I sit at the table nodding to them, pretending to be interested in their conversation, but my mind is elsewhere. I'm worried about how Claire is doing with Charlie upstairs. Although all has been quiet, Claire hasn't come back downstairs. Finally, I can't help myself.

"Jonathan, I'm going to see if Claire needs some assistance. I'll be back shortly," I announce, abruptly interrupting their business talk.

"OK. Tell Mom dessert will be served shortly."

I get to the top of the stairs, and it's eerily quiet. I peer silently into Charlie's room from the doorway. *Oh my god*. I don't believe it. Claire has a sleeping Charlie cradled in her arms. She is singing quietly to him, a soothing lullaby. Her presence here tonight makes me wonder about my own mother. I wish she could see Charlie, see how wonderful he is. She doesn't know what she's missing. Jonathan told me that she and my father didn't even bother to come to the wedding, so there is little chance she would want to meet her grandson.

Claire senses my presence and looks over her shoulder to meet my gaze. "He's asleep," she mouths to me, holding a finger up to lips. She lowers him into his crib and carefully pulls the crib sheet over him.

"He is a beautiful boy," she whispers to me when she meets me in the doorway. "Thank you," she says grabbing hold of my arm. "Jonathan is the happiest I have ever seen him. And he's so in love with you. He always has been," she says with a quiver in her voice. She looks like she is about to cry. She comes across as being very sweet-natured and is more sincere than I'd imagined she'd be.

I give her a warm smile.

"You know Anouk, Ewan is a good man. He's just old-fashioned. We never intended to interfere in your marriage. Never. I understood why you stayed in New York. You have a very successful business there. My husband, however, always had his heart set on Jonathan taking over the family business here, ever since Jonathan was very young. Please understand that we never had anything against you personally. Ewan can just be so stubborn about certain things.

I'm sorry, Anouk. I didn't mean for things to get distant between us these past two years," she says softly.

"It's OK, Claire. I can't remember the past anyway," I shrug. "What's important now is for you and Ewan to have a relationship with Charlie," I say reaching out to hold her hand.

"If you need any help with babysitting, I would like to help you with Charlie. I'm retired and have the time now," she says, her eyes wide with anticipation, awaiting my response.

"Actually, I need to attend rehab two days a week at Emory. Would you be able to mind Charlie occasionally?" I stutter.

"I would love to," she says, giving me a hug. I hug her back, relishing the comfort of her warm, motherly embrace.

* * *

CHAPTER ELEVEN
ANOUK

November 22nd, 2012
Midday

"You look nice," Jonathan says as we walk briskly to Brianna's; it's a cool, overcast day. I'm pleased that I decided to wear the blue knit sweater and jeans.

"You're not bad yourself," I say. Jonathan looks fashionable in his gray knit hooded sweater.

"You gave me this sweater for my birthday a couple of years back," he says, confidently carrying Charlie in one arm and a bottle of champagne in the other. "You're walking much better. Rehab is helping."

I nod to him as I balance the store-bought pumpkin and pecan pies in my hands and press the doorbell with my elbow. My equilibrium is still a bit off.

A short, middle-aged man in a cream-colored sweater opens the door.

"Hi, I'm Eric Sperling, Brianna's husband," he says in a friendly voice, holding out his hand to shake Jonathan's. "And you must be Anouk?" he asks, pointing a finger at me before giving me a kiss on the cheek. "Please come in. Brianna has told me *all* about you," he winks. Eric has exotic good looks; olive skin, and full lips. He places a hand up to his oiled black hair to check it's still in place.

"This is Charlie," I say.

"Please come in out of the cold and make your-selves at home. I'll take those for you," he says, taking the pies from my hand.

"Anouk! Happy Thanksgiving!" Brianna says as she pushes past Eric and kisses me on both cheeks before I can walk inside. "Oh, and you must be Jonathan. I'm Brianna. Nice to meet you," she says, holding out her hand to shake his. "Hi, Charlie. Emily is here," Brianna coos to him.

Charlie buries his head in Jonathan's neck. But Jonathan, momentarily at a loss for words, is looking at Brianna, mouth agape. He blushes like he's em-barrassed or something; that, or maybe he's stunned by her beauty. She does look drop-dead stunning in a tightly fitted black jumpsuit that shows off her full bust and the hourglass curves of her petite frame. Her glossy straight hair is down.

I nudge him with my elbow.

"Nice to meet you too, Brianna," Jonathan finally responds, giving her a sheepish smile and handing her the bottle of champagne.

"Come in, I want you to meet some of the other guests," she says, ushering us inside.

The fireplace is burning, and the house smells scrumptious—cinnamon, apple pie, and baked turkey all rolled into one heavenly aroma. Leanne, with Emily on her lap, is seated on the couch next to a burly blond man with close-set eyes, who I assume is her husband, Tony. On the couch opposite them is a formally dressed couple I don't recognize. I take Charlie from Jonathan's arms and put him on the floor.

"Anouk," Leanne says, standing up to greet me. "This is my husband Tony," she says before kissing me on the cheek.

Find your words, Anouk. "Nice to meet you, Tony. This is my husband, Jonathan," I stutter.

I have trouble finding the words to say next. I look up at Jonathan, hoping he can talk or help me in conversation, but he appears lost in thought. I don't know what's going on with him today; he seems completely preoccupied. I nudge him with my elbow again.

"Jonathan, this is Leanne and Tony." I finally get my words out.

"Err ... Nice to meet you both," he says through a forced smile.

Brianna puts her arms around me and Jonathan and walks us over to the other couple sitting silently on the couch. "Jonathan and Anouk, this is Lauren and her partner, James."

They get up from the seat and stiffly shake our hands. The woman is staring at Jonathan, mouth open as she straightens her gray suit. She looks likes she is dressed for an office meeting, not a Thanksgiving lunch.

"Hello, Jonathan," she says with a smile that doesn't reflect in her eyes.

"Lauren?" Jonathan gasps in surprise.

"You two know each other?" Brianna asks with a look of excitement.

I look at Jonathan, awaiting his explanation.

"Yes." He swallows nervously. "Um ... Lauren and I dated a long while back," he mumbles.

What the heck is she doing here?

Lauren looks down at her feet as if embarrassed, and then looks up at James out of the corner of her eye, raising an eyebrow. She then looks at Jonathan.

"Our fathers are best friends. We've known each other for years," she explains to Brianna, but her gaze doesn't leave Jonathan.

"What a small world!" Brianna exclaims in her southern drawl and placing her hands up to her mouth.

Eric returns from the kitchen carrying a silver tray of champagne flutes, each with a strawberry. He hands each guest a glass.

"Yes, it is," I mutter as I take the champagne from Eric. *This is so awkward.*

Brianna places an arm around Lauren's shoulder. "I've known Lauren for years. We studied law together at college," Brianna says.

What is the deal with all these lawyers? I look at Jonathan, and he gives me an apologetic look, shrugging one shoulder out of Lauren's view.

Just then, I feel a hand tap me.

"Anouk, I'm so pleased you made it," Leanne says, taking a sip of champagne. "I wanted to speak to you. I'm hosting the next ball committee meeting at my place next Friday. Can you make it? We'll be talking themes for the ball, and we would love your creative input. Bring Charlie," she says, bursting with enthusiasm.

"Sure."

Charlie attempts to catch Emily, who's now running around the living room. *Oh no.* Brianna's house is by no means child friendly. There are expensive decorative ornaments everywhere, and I ponder how I'm going to keep Charlie out of mischief today; it's too cold for the children to play outside.

"I may have something for the children to play with, Leanne," I say as I take Charlie's hand.

I find a few alphabet blocks in my handbag and place them on Brianna's rug for Emily and Charlie to play with.

"Thanks," Leanne sighs with relief as James comes over to talk with us.

"So you're *the* Anouk Fowler," he says, nonchalantly.

"Yes, that's me," I say with a forced smile.

"Lauren wears your designs. I wasn't aware, though, that her ex happens to be your husband," he says in a serious voice, pushing his black-framed glasses up higher on the bridge of his nose with a long finger. He has ice-blue eyes and pale skin.

"Let me guess. You're a lawyer," I quip in an attempt to direct the conversation away from me.

"No." He laughs in a stilted manner. "I'm a freelance photographer," he says, taking a sip of his champagne. He looks like the artistic type.

"What sort of photography?" I ask.

"Landscapes mostly," he says, pulling his wallet out of his back pocket.

Leanne interrupts. "James is a very talented photographer, Anouk. He has his own studio here in Atlanta, and he has also taken photos of the cars at Tony's business for advertising," she says.

"You should come into the studio next time you're in town. I can show you some of my work," James says, handing me his business card.

"OK," I say, looking over his shoulder to find Jonathan.

He's talking to Lauren by the fireplace. She's leaning against the corner of the mantelpiece, champagne in hand, gazing at him with admiration. Jonathan leans down to whisper something in her ear, and she lets out a flirtatious laugh, twirling her shoulder-length brown hair between her fingers. *Ugh!* She has cold, dark eyes, translucent skin, and thin lips. She is rather plain looking and not at all the kind of woman I imagined Jonathan would have been with before me. I'm curious to know what Jonathan is saying to her.

"Anouk," James's voice brings me back into the conversation. "If you ever need any photos taken of your designs or runway shows, I would be available."

"I'll keep that in mind, but I'm taking a break from work until next year ... until my son is older," I explain, putting his business card in my handbag. "How long have you and Lauren been married?" I ask.

"We're not married. We may as well be, though; we've been living together for a couple of years now," he says with a weak smile.

"Oh ... Do you live nearby?" I ask.

"Yes. We live only a couple of blocks from here," he says, pointing behind him.

Great. Just what I need: Jonathan's ex living two blocks away.

Brianna returns from the kitchen in a Thanksgiving-themed apron and claps her hands to get everyone's attention. "Please come take a seat at the table every-one," she calls to us before walking backward toward the formal dining room, waving her hands like a tour guide directing the tourists.

The dining table is decorated for Thanksgiving with candles and miniature gold painted pumpkins and pine cones. Brianna directs us to our seats at the table and places me and Leanne next to each other. We put the children on our laps. Jonathan takes the seat on my other side, and Tony takes the seat next to Jonathan. It doesn't take long for Jonathan to learn that Tony is a car salesman, and Jonathan is in his el-ement, asking Tony about the latest model something or other. Car talk just goes over my head. Lauren and James take their seats opposite Jonathan and Tony just as Brianna places the vegetable dishes on the table and Eric brings out the turkey.

"Everyone, I present the turkey. Brianna has made the stuffing from a secret family recipe, and over here, we have mashed potatoes, gravy, and green beans," he says pointing to the dishes on the table.

"Happy Thanksgiving, everyone. Please start. Serve yourselves," Eric announces when he finishes carving the turkey.

Eric and Brianna take their seats opposite Leanne and me.

"Jonathan, Brianna tells me that you're Ewan's son," Eric says right away. "We've known Ewan for years. How is he?" he asks as he serves himself some mashed potatoes and gravy.

"He's retiring. He had a coronary bypass, and he's handing over the reins to me at the end of the year," Jonathan replies.

"I'm sorry to hear that he's been unwell, Jonathan. Your father is well respected in Atlanta. Give him my regards," Eric says.

"Thanks, Eric. Will do," Jonathan says.

Eric and Jonathan continue to talk across the table while Leanne and I feed the children. But before long, Charlie begins whining and throwing his mashed potatoes onto the floor. Emily is doing the opposite, behaving and eating quietly on her mother's lap.

"Anouk, honey, have you thought about the design for a dress for me to wear to the ball in June? I'm thinkin' blue, pink, or white, but I'll let you decide," Brianna says as she serves herself some beans.

"I'll give the color some thought," I reply before leaning down to clean up the mashed potatoes off her cream-colored carpet. Charlie starts to cry.

"Is there somewhere I can change Charlie's diaper, Brianna?" I whisper across the table.

"Why don't you take him upstairs? Use the first room on your right," she says, pointing toward the stairs.

By the time Charlie and I return later, everyone has almost finished their meal.

"Time for pumpkin and pecan pie," Brianna says, rising from her seat.

"I'll give you a hand, Brianna. I want you to tell me the secret to making that delicious stuffing," Jonathan says. "Anouk, you finish your meal," he says, planting a kiss on my cheek before collecting our dirty plates.

Lauren watches him closely as he follows Brianna into the kitchen. But when her eyes meet mine from across the table, she shifts in her seat.

"Anouk, I wear your designs," Lauren says stony-faced. "Brianna told me you were coming today. I bought a dress from one of your stores not too long ago to wear to the ball in June."

Darn, she's coming to the ball?

She continues. "It really is a small world, Anouk. Who would have thought that you would be married to Jonathan?" she chirps. "His parents were ever so hopeful he would marry someone in the profession," she says taking a sip of champagne.

I'm unsure if she is being sincere or sarcastic, but my guess is she's mocking. The champagne has started to take effect, and since her eyes have been all over Jonathan today, I reply contemptuously, "Yes, I know. Thankfully, Jonathan came to his senses and married outside of the profession. One thing's for sure, Atlanta doesn't need another lawyer."

I laugh forcefully, looking at Eric, who chuckles, and Leanne, Tony, and James all burst into laughter.

Lauren tilts her head, purses her lips, and sits upright in her chair, straightening her suit. Her eyes squint at James with disapproval, and he quickly composes himself.

"I agree, Anouk, the last thing Brianna and I need is another lawyer in town," Eric says through a laugh.

"James, pass the champagne," Lauren scowls.

Charlie starts whining again. "I think he needs a bottle, Leanne," I say, getting up from the table to go into the kitchen to heat it up.

As I enter the kitchen, I see Jonathan cutting the pumpkin and pecan pies on the kitchen counter. Brianna's whispering something into his ear, and he nods. Charlie's cry startles them.

"Oh, hi, hon ... I was ... I was just telling Jonathan the ingredients to my turkey stuffing," she stammers. She appears flushed and embarrassed by my interruption.

"Brianna, Charlie needs to go home for a nap," I say curtly. "Thank you for your hospitality. Jonathan, we need to go—now!" I say.

"But we haven't had dessert," Brianna protests.

"I'm sorry, but we'd best go before he gets over-tired," I explain tersely.

We say our goodbyes to Eric and the guests and leave.

"Why did we have to leave so soon, Anouk?" Jonathan asks when we get to the end of the Sperlings' driveway. His eyes tighten.

He's angry with me.

"Charlie could have had a nap at Brianna's," he says with frustration.

"Where would he have slept, Jonathan?" I snap. "Are you disappointed you couldn't spend more time talking to your ex?" I mutter under my breath.

"Don't be ridiculous, Anouk," he retorts, running his hands through his hair like he always does when he's frustrated.

"What were you talking to her about? I saw you whispering in her ear at the fireplace!"

He heaves a sigh and stops walking. "I was just talking about old times," he says exasperated.

"Oh really?" I say and roll my eyes.

"Not like that, Anouk. We were just laughing about how our parents were always trying to get the two of us married, a marriage of convenience, because our fathers are best friends. She's happy for me that I'm happy … with you," he says, grabbing my arm.

"She still has eyes for you," I say, pulling out of his grasp.

"Look, I broke her heart. I wasn't in love with her, so I broke it off. I only dated her to keep Dad happy. It was years ago," he says.

"You also seemed rather cozy with Brianna in the kitchen," I say, giving him a questioning look.

"Come on, Anouk. She was just being friendly, giving me her turkey stuffing recipe. *She* was flirting with me!" he says through a laugh. He gives me one of his charismatic smiles.

"*She* was flirting with *you*?" I gasp. "I don't think so, Jonathan. I think *you* were flirting with *her*!" I tease, nudging him in his ribs. I hate how I can't stay angry with him for long.

He places Charlie on his shoulders and walks ahead, talking playfully to Charlie the length of the pebble driveway toward our house.

"Everything I've always wanted is right here … you and Charlie," he says when we get to our front door. He places a finger under my chin, forcing me to look up at him. His gaze softens. "I only have eyes for you, Anouk."

* * *

CHAPTER TWELVE

ANOUK

December 25th, 2012
Morning

It's dark. I'm yelling in anger, but I can't make out the words. I can barely see the road through the heavy rain pounding at my windshield. Someone's crying, a gut-wrenching wail ... An explosive bang, and then the sound of silence. I feel the sensation of something warm dripping down my cheek, and a metallic taste invades my mouth. There's a putrid, burning scent, and pain envelopes my stomach, a cramping, stabbing pain. My head is filled with whirring sounds. "Anouk! Anouk!" a distant, familiar voice calls my name ...

"Anouk," Jonathan's voice startles me awake. He's lying next to me in bed, eyeing me worriedly.

"It's just a dream, Anouk," he says, rubbing my arm.

"It felt so real this time," I sob. I throw my arms around him and bury my head in his chest.

"Shh," he hushes, stroking my hair off my face. "Everything is OK," he says kissing the top of my head.

I relax in his arms, comforted by the sound of his beating heart and the familiar, earthy scent of his body.

"This dream was different. I could feel the pain, and I was angry with someone." I sniff, wiping the tears from my eyes with the back of my hand.

"You could be dreaming a memory from the accident, or maybe the dream is just that ... a dream. You need to tell your therapist at Emory, OK?" he says, stroking my face. "Now, I won't have you looking so sad on Christmas Day," he adds with a wry smile.

Christmas? "It's Charlie's first Christmas!" I say, rising up off his chest.

"I have a Christmas present for you. It may cheer you up."

"Really?" I ask, surprised. "I'm sorry, I haven't bought you anything."

"Don't worry," he says. He gets out of bed and pulls a box out from under our four-poster bed. It's a present fancily wrapped in white and silver Christmas paper, topped with a silver bow.

He hands it to me with a wide grin. "Open it," he says eagerly, his eyes wide with excitement.

"You shouldn't have," I say, planting a kiss on his cheek.

I undo the wrapping paper and open the box in haste. Inside are crayons in assorted colors, drawing tools, and artist paper.

"Oh, Jonathan," I say, wiping a tear from my cheek.

"I thought it might help inspire you to design again. It won't hurt to try drawing again," he urges.

"I'll try. I will." I smile. "I can't wait for Charlie to wake up so we can give him our presents," I say, hand combing my bed hair back into place. It's 7:00 a.m., and Charlie is still sound asleep. Last night, we put Charlie's presents under the Christmas tree. We bought him a little red trike with a handle and a first Christmas teddy bear that plays a recording of me saying "Merry Christmas, Charlie" when you squeeze its tummy.

"What time do we need to be at your folks' place for Christmas lunch?" I ask.

"Midday. So we have plenty of time," he says with a seductive grin, looking at me out of the corner of his eye. "I think we should make use of the time to ourselves,"

"What did you have in mind?" I ask, running my hand across his chest.

"You. *You* are always on my mind. I think it's my turn to unwrap my Christmas present now, don't you?" he asks, pulling at my nightdress and biting his bottom lip as he inches his body closer to mine. "Charlie's asleep," he says, raising an eyebrow.

I let out a chuckle, amused by his attempts to seduce me. For someone who has just woken, he looks sexy. He runs a hand through his hair to push it off his face, flexing a bicep, then leans in to kiss me. *He's an Adonis, a perfect man. How did I get so lucky?*

I hold his head in my hands as I kiss him back. His earthy scent and the feeling of his soft lips against mine unleash a feeling that I hadn't felt with him before—lust.

I slide my hand down his chest toward his boxers. He lets out a faint groan and proceeds to take off my nightdress before we are interrupted by an ear-piercing shriek; Charlie's distressing cry blares through the baby monitor on my bedside table, startling us.

"I'll go to him," I say breathlessly, jumping out of bed to race down the hall into Charlie's bedroom. Charlie is standing in his crib, crying, his mouth gaping and his eyes wide with a look of terror. It's a look I've never before seen on Charlie's face.

"Shhh," I say to him as I pick him up out of his crib to hold him tight, close to my chest. I bounce him in my arms for a while, but he doesn't settle, so I carry him downstairs to make him a bottle.

"Jonathan!" I scream when I get closer to the base of the staircase. *Oh my god*!

"What is it?" he asks, panicked, when he gets to Charlie and me in the foyer.

"The front door is open," I say, pointing.

"What?!" His brow furrows. Jonathan strokes Charlie on the back of his head before he goes straight out the door, sprinting into the front yard to take a look around.

Charlie stops crying when he sees Jonathan come back in a short time later and locks the front door behind him. Jonathan has a look of relief.

"I must have left the front door open behind me last night when I brought in Charlie's trike out of the car," he says, scratching his head in reflection.

"Are you sure?" I ask with a questioning look.

Jonathan follows me as I go around the house to check all the rooms. Our belongings appear untouched.

"I'm positive that I left the front door open, OK?" he says as he follows me into our bedroom.

"Jonathan, I think someone was in the house."

* * *

CHAPTER THIRTEEN
ANOUK

April 3rd, 2013
Morning

The flowers in the garden have started to bloom from the arrival of the spring sunshine. I am studying them from my attic window, hoping they can give me some kind of creative inspiration. *How on earth am I going to design a dress?* Brianna is still persistent in wanting me to design an evening dress for her to wear at the annual Children's Charity Ball in June.

My study is well set up now. The walls of the attic are covered by six canvas paintings of flowers in a variety of colors. My study shelves are stocked with fashion magazines, awards, photos, and articles, and I have my new desk stocked with the paper, crayons, and drawing tools that Jonathan bought me for Christmas.

I pull out some fashion magazines and have a flick through them in the hope they'll kickstart some creativity. *Shit!* I throw the magazines on the floor in a huff, inadvertently startling Charlie. *Darn.* The magazines may not have provided much inspiration, but I pull out some paper and start to draw anyway. Brianna had said she wanted a dress in blue, pink, or white. *Hmm.* I start drawing, and for no particular reason, sketch out a floor-length, long-sleeved, fitted dress. *Not bad, Anouk.*

I spend the morning drawing and end up with at least another five dress designs in different styles and lengths.

"Ma ... ma," a little voice beside me calls, holding onto my chair. Charlie has been such a good boy, quietly playing with crayons next to me all this time.

"Let me get you something to eat," I say, picking him up and kissing him on his crayon-smeared cheek. I hold his hand firmly as he takes cautious steps down the stairs that lead to the kitchen. I make him a sandwich, then put him in his crib with his bottle for his daily nap and go back up to the attic to finish the designs for Brianna. The sketches aren't perfect, but they're not bad for a first attempt. I need to decide on the color. I'm not convinced that white or pink will work for these designs; they could make the dresses look too bridal.

At the ball committee meeting at Leanne's place, we all agreed upon an "Under the Sea" theme for the ball, so blue would work nicely, the color of the ocean. *Yes, that would work.* I color the designs in blue and hold them up against the light coming through the attic window. One of the first designs I did looks nearly identical to the royal blue dress I wore on the night I met Jonathan. *That's it!* Brianna can borrow my dress. It's a size four, so it should fit her petite frame perfectly. It's only been worn once, and she would look stunning in it. Besides, it doesn't fit me anymore.

As I rise from my chair to go look at the dress, a flash of movement outside the attic window catches my eye. I see someone running from the direction of our library, below, heading across the front lawn toward our driveway; the same visitor in the black hooded sweatshirt that I saw last year. *Who is that?*

Without caution, I race downstairs to the front door barefoot, and I fling it open to run out onto our driveway, following them. I can see the person's back now, this mysterious stranger dressed in matching black sweatpants, with the hood of their sweatshirt up over their head. They're halfway up our driveway, heading toward the street.

I run as fast as I am able toward them down the long driveway, my feet hurting from the sharpness of the pebbles digging and clacking between my toes. I keep losing traction, but I get close enough for them to hear me as they race closer to the street.

"Hey!" I yell breathlessly, at the top of my lungs.

They slow their pace at the sound of my voice and turn their head slightly to the left, without fully turning around. I can't see a profile, but I can just make out the tip of a nose. It could be a teenager; they're about my height.

"What do you want?" I demand.

They stop dead in their tracks. I realize in this moment that I could be in danger. I don't know if this person is armed or dangerous, so I stop running. I glance back at the house, gauging the distance to the open front door, just in case they turn to come at me. I judge that I can make it back into the house before they could reach me. I get ready to turn, just in case, but they just stand there, silent and motionless in the middle of the driveway with their back to me, arms dangling by their side. A feeling of panic washes over me. I don't feel safe. Charlie and I are home alone. A chill sends shivers up my spine at the thought of someone hurting Charlie.

"What do you want?" I ask again. I wait a second or two for a response, but there is no reply. I call out again. "Who are you?"

But they bolt, running faster than they had before, and they're now close to where our driveway ends.

"Stay away from us, you hear me?" I shout as they disappear onto the street. "Stay away!"

I go back in the house, lock the front door, and race upstairs to check on Charlie. He's still sound asleep, undisturbed, and I go back downstairs to locate Detective Mantle's card. He is quick to respond, arriving alone not long after I report what happened to him. I didn't want to disturb Jonathan at work.

I invite Detective Mantle into the living room and take a seat opposite him as he opens his notepad and pulls a pen out of his shirt pocket. His demeanor is serious. "So, you said on the phone that you saw someone dressed in black running away from the house, up your driveway toward the street?" he asks with a questioning look.

"Yes, I was upstairs when I saw them from the attic window, coming from the library," I point.

"Can you describe their appearance?" he asks, pursing his thin lips.

"They were wearing a black hooded sweatshirt, matching sweatpants, lean body, about my height."

"Did you see their face?" he asks, taking notes.

"No, they had their back to me, and the hood of their sweatshirt was up over their face."

"And you think this person has been watching *you*?" He frowns.

"Yes. I saw the same person last year, just after we moved in. I'm sure I saw them watching me from the library window," I say, my voice frantic.

"Did you actually *see* someone watching you from the window?"

"No, well, I sensed it, someone watching me when I was picking up the moving boxes in the library. I saw movement at the window from out of the corner of my eye, and when I went outside, I saw the same person I saw today, running out onto the street, just like today."

"Has Jonathan seen this mystery person?" he asks, frowning again.

"No, he's been at work on both occasions," I sigh.

"Mrs. Fowler, I'm not doubting that you saw someone running along your driveway, but it doesn't prove that they were watching you." Detective Mantle's eyes narrow and he tilts his head.

I can't help but feel he doesn't believe me, that he's skeptical about what I'm telling him.

"I know someone is watching me, Detective; I'm sure of it. I forgot to mention, I saw a figure standing outside our house in the dark early one morning. I'm convinced someone is stalking me," I say.

He shifts in his seat, closing his notepad and putting his pen away in his shirt pocket. His eyes soften. "Look, I would make sure you keep the house locked when you're home. Be vigilant, just in case someone *is* trying to break in. There have been a few break-ins several blocks over," he says. His eyes dart around the living room. "You do have some expensive collectibles that someone might want to steal," he nods. A smile appears on his thin lips. "I'll make a report when I get back to the station, OK?" he reassures.

I nod, wiping a tear from my cheek with the back of my hand.

"Now, I need to ask you, since I last saw you, can you recall anything about the events that occurred on the evening of June fifteenth last year?"

"Not really, but I had a nightmare about the accident. I was yelling at someone, I don't know why," I say, shaking my head. "And someone was calling my name. It's hazy, and that's all I can remember."

"OK, well you have my number. Call me if you remember anything or need anything else," he says, as he rises from his seat to leave.

* * *

I tell Jonathan everything that happened when he gets home from work. He is pleased I called Detective Mantle right away.

"I'll stay home with you and Charlie tomorrow," Jonathan says.

"I can't shake this feeling that someone is watching *me*," I say. "I don't feel safe in this house anymore."

"Everything's going to be OK. I'll work from home all week if I have to. I'm not going to let anything happen to you or Charlie, I promise," he says, placing his hand on my shoulder. "If you feel ready, maybe you could go spend a couple of days in New York. You know, get out of the house and go visit your office."

"What about Charlie?" I ask.

"Charlie will be fine. I'll take good care of him. It would only be for a couple of days, Anouk. Charlie is older now."

"OK, I'll go. I need to speak to Tom anyway."

* * *

CHAPTER FOURTEEN
ANOUK

April 4th, 2013
Morning

I attend my usual early morning rehabilitation appointment with Annette before flying out on a direct flight to New York. Jonathan called Ewan yesterday evening to say he would work from home for the next two days so he could look after Charlie, then he booked my flight to New York after he spoke to Tom. Jonathan said Tom was thrilled to hear I was going to visit the office today, especially since Tom is due to fly out to London the day after tomorrow.

I drank too much wine last night. Jonathan in particular has been drinking more than usual lately, at home and socially. Since Thanksgiving, Brianna,

Leanne, and I have started taking turns hosting monthly dinner parties. We have been enjoying our new friendships in Atlanta, and it's been easy to settle in with such a supportive social network of close friends who live nearby.

I lie back on the reclined seat in business class and try to visualize what Tom is like. I wonder what we talked about, how close we were, and I'm curious to understand why he hasn't contacted me since the accident. Jonathan has shown me photos of Tom and told me countless stories of our times together. I'm sure Tom can give me some of the answers I need. It feels strange meeting the supposed "best friend" I can't remember.

I was careful not to comment on Tom's looks when Jonathan showed me the photos of me and Tom together; I couldn't help but find him attractive. Jonathan doesn't appear jealous of our relationship, which may be due to the fact that Jonathan is absolutely convinced Tom is gay. When I quizzed Jonathan about it, he said he'd formed his opinion because of the way Tom dressed, along with the fact that Tom hasn't had a girlfriend in the past eight years. Go figure.

I land in New York and catch a cab to the Garment District, and a short time later, the cab pulls up at Designite Fashion House on Fifth Avenue. My senses are overwhelmed by the sights and smells of

New York City, the huge number of people going about their daily business, the smell of exhaust fumes, and the urgent sounds of the city. I feel somewhat uneasy; I've become accustomed to the quiet life on our street in Atlanta. I pay the driver and get out of the cab with ease, thanks to my rehabilitation exercises.

I feel my heart pounding as I step into the elevator on the ground floor and adjust my hair in the mirror. Then I press the elevator button with a shaking finger.

On the twelfth floor, I step out of the elevator. There are glass doors about eleven feet in front of me with etched signage: **DESIGNITE FASHION HOUSE**. As I open one of the doors, a flash of a memory hits me like a lightning bolt. *I remember these glass doors.* I become breathless with anxiety. *Get it together, Anouk.* I take a deep breath and compose myself. Behind the glass door, I'm greeted by a twenty-something, red-haired receptionist sitting behind a long glass desk.

She rises from her seat as she says, "Hello, Anouk, welcome back," in a sincere tone, but she doesn't crack a smile. She is tall and leggy and could easily pass for a model in her ivy-green pinafore dress.

"Hello, you are ... ?" I ask.

"Amy. Amy Jones," she says holding out her hand to shake mine.

"Of course. Amy, how are you?" I ask, pretending I actually know who she is. She raises an eyebrow, and her mouth gapes slightly. Maybe she's surprised that I didn't know her name.

"I'm very well. Tom is expecting you," she says matter-of-factly and without a smile. She picks up the phone on her desk and dials. "Tom, Anouk is here," she says.

"He'll be right with you," she says, hanging up the phone. "Can I get you a coffee, tea, or a glass of water?" she asks in an almost robotic tone of voice.

"No. I'm fine."

I look around the reception area; it's not what I'd expected. It's almost sterile in all white, with a white leather couch. The only splashes of color are the green stems of the seven white lilies in a tall glass vase on Amy's desk and Amy's ivy-green dress. A couple of young women walk into the reception area, chatting excitedly like schoolgirls. They stop in their tracks when they see me, give me a cautious smile, bow their heads, and scurry quietly up the hall. I hear footsteps clicking on the tiled white floors. *It must be Tom.*

"Nouk! It's so good to see you!" he says as he runs toward me and proceeds to wrap me in a bear hug that feels like he just squeezed all the oxygen out of my lungs. *He smells good.*

"Hi ... Tom?" I rasp as I try to catch my breath. *He's huge.*

"Wow, Nouk. You look great!" he says, grabbing my limp right hand as his eyes look me up and down.

He's probably noticed I've put on weight. He's better looking in person than in the photos Jonathan has shown me. It's hard not to notice his muscular physique under his tightly fitted gray suit and collared white shirt. He must be at least six-three. There's not a blond hair out of place, thanks to all the hair product. He looks like he could be in his late thirties, early forties. I can't tell.

He turns to Amy. "Hold all calls for the next two hours," he says in an authoritative voice, and she nods in reply.

"Let's go into my office, Nouk," he says, placing a gentle hand on my back to guide me.

"Nice to see you, Amy." I wave as I walk away.

She stares at me blankly as I follow Tom down the hallway. In his office, he pulls out a chair for me and proceeds to take a seat at his desk. His office is immaculate and also minimalistic, with floor-to-ceiling windows that look out across New York City, a glass desk, and an iron bookshelf taking up an entire wall that is well organized with photos, fashion magazines, awards, and books.

"So, how are you doing, Nouk?" he asks, loosening his thin black tie as he wipes a few drops of sweat from his forehead with the back of his hand.

He appears as nervous as I am. "I'm well. Feeling better each day. I still have trouble with my speech, but I'm getting there," I stutter nervously, looking around his office.

"Are you enjoying Atlanta?"

"Um … So far, I like it," I say quietly.

"I never would have thought it, Nouk, that you of all people would ever leave New York," he says with a sardonic laugh, flashing a set of perfectly straight teeth.

I don't know how to respond, so I just ignore the comment and give him a forced smile. It's so frustrating to have what feels like complete strangers know more about me than I know about myself. Jonathan told me that Tom was always direct and that he had a wonderful sense of humor, so perhaps he's just being playful.

"We've missed you so much. *I've* missed you," he says in a now-sincere voice.

"Thanks. Um … look, Tom, I'm so sorry I can't remember our relationship or anything about the business. Jonathan has told me all about you though," I smile. *Say it, Anouk.* "He says we were like best friends." *Awkward.*

I immediately pick up a framed photo of us off his desk, awaiting his reaction. Actually, there are at least three photos of us with Mia at fashion events in his office. There aren't photos of anything else. I have an immediate urge to ask him right away about Mia, but I decide to hold off. I want to get reacquainted with him first. I'm in New York until tomorrow, so there's plenty of time to ask, and I'm curious to see if he will mention her first.

"We were best friends. I hope we still are, Nouk," he says with a hint of sadness in his blue eyes. "I'm so sorry, Nouk, about what happened to you. Jonathan called me numerous times immediately after the car accident, and he said you weren't able to speak. He later told me about the possibility of long-term amnesia. He said you had a severe head injury and it wasn't appropriate for me to visit at the hospital or at home. Which was completely understandable ... I knew you would contact me when you were ready," he sighs, giving me a weak smile.

That explains why he hasn't called me.

He gets up and walks over to the floor-to-ceiling windows. He's talking to me, but his gaze is directed out the window. "Jonathan made it very clear to me a few days after your accident that I should focus on the business and take over temporarily as CEO, given that ..." He trails off mid-sentence like he's deep in thought about something. His round face appears forlorn.

He closes his eyes for a second or two and bites his bottom lip, almost as though he was about to say something that he shouldn't have. Perhaps he doesn't want to upset me by talking about Mia or the accident. I'm not sure, so I quickly end the uncomfortable silence.

"Jonathan explained that it was what I would have wanted, for you to take over as acting CEO. Jonathan is protective. He didn't think it was appropriate for me to have visitors. He thought I wouldn't have wanted others seeing me like that in the hospital. He showed me the photos of myself just after the accident, and to be honest, it wasn't pretty," I stammer.

"Of course. I understand … Well, you're still very pretty, Nouk," he says straight-faced, tilting his head to one side.

He goes quiet, looks down at his feet, then looks back out the window, distant in thought.

This is so awkward. I abruptly change the subject. "So tell me what's happening with the business," I ask assertively.

I'm pleased I had the foresight to meet him in the morning when my speech is at its best.

He sits back in his chair behind the desk. "Yes, of course. Well, as a matter of fact, sales are at an all-time high since the launch of our spring collection. Sales have increased by thirty percent," he says proudly, leaning back in his chair.

"Wow, Tom; that's great news … What do you think has contributed to the uplift?" I ask, trying to sound intelligent, like I actually know something about business—*my* business.

"Well, as Jonathan may have already told you, I hired a new marketing and public relations guru,

Adam Black, along with two new designers, Chloe Cooper and Alison Clarkson. I want you to meet them while you're here. Chloe and Alison can take most of the credit. They're young, work well together as a cohesive team, and they have fresh and creative designs. Our customers are telling us they love the new designs," he says with a look of satisfaction.

"Oh, that's fantastic, Tom. I'm sure it's also due to your creative direction."

His face flushes, and he grins broadly. He appears pleased by my flattery.

"I have so many questions I need to ask you. And I think you're the best person to answer the questions I have," I say.

He studies my face for a moment and leans forward in his chair. "I'm sure you do. Look, why don't I reintroduce you to the team, and then I'll take you for a coffee, and you can ask away. Gee, you're so different, Nouk," he says as he gets out of his chair and walks toward his office door, indicating for me to follow. Tom walks me through the office and introduces me to the staff and Chloe, Alison, and Adam in their respective offices. They all shake my hand, and each tells me they're honored to work for me. It feels very strange indeed; they're treating me like a celebrity.

Afterward, Tom takes me to a retro coffee shop on Fifth Avenue. I take a seat next to the window so I can see people going about their daily business across

New York City. He proceeds to order two cappuccinos from the waitress without asking me what type of coffee I want and how I have it. I guess he would know how I like my coffee after working for me all these years.

"So ... what do you want to know?" he asks, placing a smooth, well-manicured hand on top of mine. Everything about Tom is polished; he has a metrosexual, masculine beauty.

"How long have we known each other?" I ask.

"Eight years, nearly nine." He smiles.

"So how did we first meet?"

"I was working at another fashion house, and you headhunted me, offered me nearly twice as much as what I was earning there. I accepted your offer, and I've worked for you ever since."

"Tom, how come I don't seem to have many friends?"

"Nouk ..." he pauses, momentarily pursing his full lips and cocking his head to one side. He continues, "I wasn't expecting that question! Um ... quite simply, you didn't have time for friends," he says matter-of-factly.

"Really? But I was friends with you, right?" I ask with a questioning look.

"Yes, Nouk, but I worked with you, so that made it reasonable for you to justify our friendship," he says, crossing his arms and placing his elbows on the table.

Is he being sarcastic? "So are you saying that we wouldn't be friends if we hadn't worked together?"

"No. I'm not saying that at all. We both like the same things, we were creative together, we socialized and went to the gym together. We had a lot in common, and it was easy for us to be friends. We were both ambitious. You were very selective about your friendships because your career and Designite Fashion House were always the priorities and you didn't want any distractions." He shrugs.

That doesn't sound like me at all! I really like my new friends in Atlanta. "Did people want to be my friend?" I murmur.

His gaze moves out the window, like he's distant in thought.

Thanks for the reassurance. "Please, Tom. I need you to be completely honest with me. It may help," I plead.

His eyes are now on mine. "Well … err … to be honest, no, you were difficult to get to know; let's put it that way," he says.

Tom shifts in his seat. I can tell that he is uncomfortable with this conversation. The waitress arrives with our coffee.

"Why was I difficult to get to know?" I ask.

"Well, you certainly didn't suffer fools gladly, that's for sure. Some people may have perceived you as being ambitious, conceited, aloof. You didn't make conversation with the staff like you did this morning with Amy." He snorts with laughter.

That doesn't sound like me at all. "You mean the red-headed fembot at reception?" I retort.

Tom almost chokes with laughter, inhaling some of his coffee as he lets out a loud, hearty guffaw. "It's great to see that you still have your wicked sense of humor. That's exactly what you would've said twelve months ago. Amy nearly fell off her chair when you said it was nice to see her. You've never spoken to her like that ... *never*," he says, still chuckling.

"That explains why she looked so shocked when I asked her how she was. Not that I can even remember her," I scoff.

"You've never asked any of the staff how they were. You hired Amy. You wanted her on reception because she looked like a model and would be a great clothes horse to wear our designs at the front of the house. She's one of our best employees, by the way," he says, now serious.

"Did she like me?" I ask, almost sounding desperate.

"Most of the staff don't like you, but they respect you, admire you, and want to work for you ... Geez, Nouk, you really *are* different. Previously, you wouldn't have cared what others may have thought," he says, studying my face.

"You make me sound like a complete bitch," I say, stirring my coffee.

"Some people thought you were. You're a clever bitch, though," he says with a cheeky grin.

I feel relaxed in Tom's company. He is easy to talk to, and I'm starting to understand why we are good friends.

"Tell me, how am I different?" I ask.

"For starters, I've never seen you turn up at the office in jeans and a T-shirt," he says, pointing to my clothing. "Secondly, you appear happier, calmer … relaxed," he says casually, shrugging his shoulders.

"I like wearing jeans and T-shirts now. I like casual. It may come as a surprise to you, but I have absolutely no idea at all about fashion at present."

"Yeah, well, that's obvious. I'll have to do something about that," he quips, flashing me a broad grin before taking another sip of his coffee.

I like his playfulness and his directness. I'm enjoying our banter. He makes it easy for me to be just as direct with him.

"So tell me about you. Do you have a girlfriend?" I ask him from out of the blue. I want to find out if what Jonathan said about him is true.

"No. I don't," he says in a low voice. He shifts in his seat. His eyes dart from mine to the street outside the window as he takes a sip of his coffee.

"Why?" I ask bluntly. *I can't believe I just blurted that out.*

His eyes are now on mine.

"First, I don't have time for a girlfriend because I'm too damned busy working. And second, you're already taken," he says flatly.

What did he just say? Jonathan said he was gay. I feel my heart racing again, and there's a tightness in my chest. I flush and give him a wry smile. I don't know if I'm flattered by the comment or offended, so I nervously stir my coffee, thinking about how I should respond. Thankfully, he is quick to fill the uncomfortable silence.

"I just say it how it is. It's true." His eyes are fixed on mine so intensely that it feels like they're piercing my soul. He places his large hand on mine.

"How is your relationship with Jonathan going, anyway?" he asks in a sympathetic tone.

I pause, momentarily blindsided by his question. "We're good ... Why?" I ask, now defensive. *My marriage is none of your business.*

"Oh, no reason. You told me on a couple of occasions that your marriage was strained at times," he says sheepishly.

What on earth is he talking about? "We're very happy, actually, which is quite amazing considering what we've been through in the past year. But, you know, having a child together has probably made us closer," I say, stirring my coffee.

I look up at Tom. He's gone quiet. His face is blank, and he's staring at his coffee like he's distant in thought again. All color is drained from his face.

"Are you OK?" I ask, placing my hand on his; it feels clammy.

He pulls his hand away and quickly says, "Uh ... I'm so sorry, Anouk. I don't feel well. I think I've had *way* too much coffee today." He places the back of his hand on his forehead and gives me a forced smile.

"Can I get you a glass of water or something?"

"No, Nouk. I might go back to the office to collect a few things, and then I'll head home early."

"Well, OK. If you're all right, I'll go check into the hotel. I'm going to start spending more time in New York, Tom. My therapist and Jonathan think it would be good for me to get back into my old routine."

He reaches out to my left hand and holds it between his hands.

"It would be great to have you back on board, but only when you feel ready. OK?" he says, rising from his seat.

"Let me walk you back to the office."

"No, seriously, I'm fine. You go check into your hotel," he says, patting me on my arm.

"Tom, are you sure you're OK?"

"Yes. I'll pick up the tab for the coffee, and I'll see you tomorrow, all right?"

"Well, can you at least text me tonight to let me know you're OK? Please?" I plead.

"Will do. It's been wonderful seeing you," he says with a warm smile and proceeds to give me another one of his bear hugs.

I kiss him on the cheek and step outside to hail a cab.

* * *

CHAPTER FIFTEEN
ANOUK

April 5th, 2013
Morning

It's blurry through the rain, but I see it; the shadowy figure standing motionless on the road in the dark. It can't see me. It turns in my direction for a brief moment before running into the darkness ...

I wake up breathless in the hotel room. *Oh my god.* The dream felt so real, so vivid.

It's just a dream, I reassure myself as I get out of bed and get dressed. I've got to meet Tom at the office. I check my cell phone for any messages from him, but he hasn't texted. I'll have to assume he's feeling better today. Jonathan called me last night after he put Charlie to bed to let me know they're OK. He said he was going to open a bottle of wine and do some work. I begged him not to drink, just in case he had to attend to Charlie during the night, and he promised he'd only have one glass.

At the office, I'm greeted at reception by Amy, who is wearing a baby blue dress.

"Hi, Anouk. Good to see you again," she says with warmth in her pale blue eyes this time around. "Tom will be with you soon, or you can go down to his office," she says as she gets up from her desk, twirling her long hair between her fingers and pointing toward Tom's office.

"Thanks, Amy. I'll surprise him," I say giving her a wink. She seems taken aback by my gesture, standing there, mouth agape when I turn to give her a wave as I walk down the hall to Tom's office. I can hear Tom talking quietly to someone when I reach his office door, and I stand outside for a moment to listen to his conversation.

"I understand. Rest assured, I won't say a word about it, Jonathan. You too, and thanks for the call. Speak soon," I hear Tom say.

Why is Jonathan calling Tom? Won't say a word about what? I appear in the office doorway and tap lightly on the door. Tom looks up from his desk.

"Nouk! Come in," he says in a welcoming voice. "Shut the door behind you," he says as he gets up from his desk and gives me one of his tight bear hugs, pressing me into his white linen shirt.

"Hi, Tom." I say with bated breath. He smells like he is fresh from taking a shower.

"You look fantastic! I always said red was your color … I haven't seen you wear that suit in a while," he says as he looks me up and down.

I'm pleased that I made a conscious decision to dress in a suit today. After all, I am the owner of a fashion house, so it's only fitting that I should start looking like one.

"Thank you." I blush. He doesn't appear nervous today. "Feeling better … I hope. There is work to be done, you know," I tease, tapping my finger on his desk.

"Yes, thank you, and it's great to see you still have your sense of humor."

I don't feel as nervous today visiting Tom. I do feel like I've known him for years, and I relax in his company.

"I just got off the phone with Jonathan, actually. He wanted to talk business, and I promised him that you would text him to let him know you're OK. He worries about you, Anouk," he says with a look of concern.

"Yes, I know. Jonathan is overprotective. I spoke to him last night, but I'll text him now, OK?" I sigh, annoyed by the mollycoddling from the two of them.

I pull out my cell phone and quickly text Jonathan, who responds almost immediately with a selfie of him and Charlie and the caption, *Enjoying boy time, X.*

"So, you're off to London tomorrow?" I ask, putting my phone away.

"Yes. I'm going to be on a roadshow for the next few weeks promoting our spring collection. I think we can expand our presence in the UK market," he reveals.

"Have we done that before? Promoted our brand overseas, that is?" I ask.

"Yes. In fact, you and I have been to London together," he says, getting up from behind his desk and walking over to the iron bookshelf, where he retrieves a framed photo. "This is you and me at London fashion week in two thousand eleven," he says, handing it to me.

"And Mia," I say, pointing at her in the photograph.

It's a picture of Tom, Mia, and me walking down a runway. The three of us are holding hands, dressed in our finest. I look quite glamorous in an emerald green dress. My blonde hair was longer, and I look younger; I've aged.

"Can you remember her?" he recoils, startled by my declaration.

"No. I only found out about her from the Atlanta police when they gave me an unexpected visit last year and told me about her death. It would have been nice to hear about her from you or Jonathan," I retort.

"Err … About that, Anouk," he says, scratching his head. "I'm sorry you had to find out that way. Jonathan told me this morning that the police told you, and he asked me not to bring it up. We should've told you sooner, but we'd agreed that we wouldn't upset you. We were going to tell you when the time was right. We just had your best interests at heart."

"Jonathan should have told me," I say, annoyed. I hand him back the photo.

"Look, Jonathan wanted you to settle into Atlanta, and then *he* was going to tell you. He didn't want to overwhelm you. I promise," he says sincerely.

He has a look of innocence, and I just know he's telling the truth. "What was she like? Tell me all about her," I ask impatiently.

"Mia was a *very* talented designer. She was beautiful. You can see that," he says, pointing to the photograph. "Although she wasn't born looking like that. She had *a lot* of plastic surgery and lost a considerable amount of weight. She could be funny, quickwitted, and generous, but she could be volatile too. She could be both fire and ice, and she was street smart. Anouk, she loved this company. It became her life, and she worked extremely hard for you."

"What was our relationship like?" I ask.

"You were the business brains, and she had the flair for design. I won't lie, Anouk … your relationship was at times tumultuous, and you had creative differences. You were opposites in many ways, but you had a working chemistry that just … clicked. Together, you were like yin and yang. Without her, your brand wouldn't be where it is today," he says matter-of-factly.

"Were we close friends?" I ask.

He pauses momentarily, reflective. "Yes, you were. You became friends at design school, where you took pity on her. She had a rough childhood. She never liked to talk about it. You took her under your wing and let her stay with you rent-free. You always looked out for her. Mia was extremely grateful for that, and she always tried her best to please you. She would've done anything for you," he says with a hint of sadness in his eyes.

"What about her partner, her child?"

"I never met her partner nor the kid. She was tight-lipped about her private life. We were close, but she never really confided in me that way."

He pauses, sliding his finger over her photo, caressing it, before placing it carefully back on the shelf. He looks forlorn when he turns to me.

"She did have quite a few different on-again, off-again relationships with men, and I met a couple over the years. The last relationship I knew of was with some male model she met at a fashion show, but nothing ever long term. Her father called me shortly after her death and explained that the family were having a family-only funeral in Philadelphia. I was told outright that we weren't invited, and when I asked about the kid, he said he and his wife were going to raise their grandson." He shrugs.

"Oh my god. Tom, I feel awful. I was following her that night, and my car hit hers. I feel responsible for her death," I say.

"It wasn't your fault, OK?" he says, placing a reassuring hand on my shoulder.

"How do you know? Do you know why was I following her that night? Jonathan said I told him I was heading straight home from work," I say, getting up and starting to pace. I feel a tightness in my chest.

"I don't know why you were following her. The night of the car accident, I was out of the state on business. Please relax. Sit down, and I'll get you a bottle of water," he says, walking over to a fridge behind his desk. "Here," he says, passing me the water. "It's probably just a coincidence that you were driving at the same time on the same road," he says, taking a seat behind his desk.

"The Atlanta police told me that you spoke to the NYPD. What did you tell them?" I ask, taking a sip of water.

"Not much. I told them that you were my boss, had a car accident where you were seriously injured and that you moved to Atlanta with your husband. I gave them your address in Atlanta. I told them I'd temporarily taken over as CEO during your recovery. Oh, and they did mention that they may need to look at our books in the future," he adds nonchalantly, shrugging his shoulders.

"Why would they want to look over our books?" I ask, defensive.

"I don't know," he says, getting himself a bottle of water from the fridge.

"It felt like I . . ." *Get your words out, Anouk!* "It felt like I was being investigated. I felt … interrogated," I stammer.

"I wouldn't worry, Nouk. The police are probably just following protocol. Besides, our books are up-to-date, thanks to Amy's excellent bookkeeping skills. She's not just a pretty face," he chuckles, raising an eyebrow. I can tell he's trying to lighten the mood.

"Yes, well, I did get a warmer reception from her this morning," I chuckle.

"See, she's not a fembot after all," he says through a laugh, flashing his perfect teeth. His smile relaxes me. He has a boyish charm, and he appears completely oblivious to his attractiveness.

I give him a wry smile.

"There you go; there's your old smile," he beams. "How 'bout we change the subject," he says, taking a seat. "I want to take you to the studio so you can have a look over next season's collection, and then we can grab some lunch."

"Yes, please." I'm starting to feel queasy, and I don't know if it's the conversation or because I'm missing Charlie.

After Tom shows me the designs, we walk downtown to the retro coffee shop on Fifth Avenue where he took me yesterday. It's bustling and noisy with twenty- and thirty-somethings this time. He finds a quiet nook in the back of the shop, and we take a seat next to each other. A blonde waitress comes over to our table and hands us menus.

"Hey, you're Anouk Fowler," the young waitress says, pointing her finger at me. "I love your designs. Can I get an autograph?" she asks, handing me her pen and a paper napkin from her apron pocket.

I look at her blankly. Then I look at Tom, and he gives me a reassuring nod. *Crap!* I inch closer to him and whisper under my breath. "I don't know *how* to sign my name. I can't remember."

"Just write your initials," he whispers back, giving the waitress a reassuring smile.

"Sure," I say to her before writing my initials on the napkin. I hand it to her.

"Thank you. I really appreciate it," she says, wide-eyed.

"Get used to it. You're famous, you know," Tom mutters into my ear too quietly for the waitress to hear.

I must admit, it felt good not being anonymous for a change. I could get used to this kind of attention.

"Can I get two cappuccinos, please?" Tom asks.

"Sure. I'll be back shortly to take your lunch order."

"That felt so strange, Tom, being recognized," I laugh when she's gone.

He chuckles at my childlike reaction. "Like I said, you're famous," he smiles. "Do you know how hard it was for Amy and me to field inquiries from a few persistent journalists and photographers wanting to know what had happened to you and hounding us for your contact info?" He sighs. "Jonathan changed your phone numbers and arranged for the hospital to give you a pseudonym during your recovery. Amy and I would say that you were on an extended holiday in the Bahamas to spend time with family." He laughs. "Hopefully that put them off your and Jonathan's scent for a while."

"Thanks, Tom. We haven't been hounded by the media."

"Good," he says, placing a hand on mine.

"But I have had a few unsettling visits from some-one standing outside our house. This person's been watching me. I saw glimpses of them outside the house, but I didn't see their face."

"It could be the media," he says. "It wouldn't sur-prise me what they're capable of doing in order to get a picture of you. Be careful."

"Of course, that makes complete sense now, that it could be the media."

"So, tell me about you, Anouk. How's mother-hood?"

"Great. I love being a mom. Charlie is wonderful," I gush. "Tom, you mentioned yesterday that I told you my marriage was strained at times. Tell me, what exactly did I tell you?"

"You said on a couple of occasions that you and Jonathan were having problems because Jonathan was constantly hounding you to have kids. You didn't want them because you wanted to focus on your career."

"One of the only memories that I can recall is when I told Jonathan I was pregnant. It's sketchy, but Jonathan didn't exactly appear happy when I told him that," I say, confused.

"Are you serious, Anouk?" He frowns. "Jonathan would've been over the moon. He is so head over heels in love with you. All he's ever wanted was to start a family with you," he says, frustration in his tone. He leans back on the couch.

"I wish I could remember." I sigh.

"Are you ready to order lunch?" the waitress interrupts, placing our coffees on the table.

"Can we get two BLTs on whole wheat bread, toasted, with salad on the side, hold the fries, and two iced teas, please," he asks the waitress.

I glare at Tom, mouth gaping. I don't know if I'm impressed with his choices or offended by his assumption that I wanted him to order on my behalf.

"What?" he asks, unfazed, shrugging his shoulders at my reaction. "I've worked with you for years. I know what you like to eat," he says, taking a sip of his coffee and giving me a cheeky grin.

"Ha ha," I quip sarcastically. I'm interrupted by the vibration of my cell phone, and I pull it out of my pocket. "It's Jonathan," I mouth to Tom, holding a finger to my lips for him to be quiet so I can hear.

"Hi, Jonathan," I answer.

There is no response but heavy, jagged breathing.

"Jonathan? Hello, Jonathan? Are you OK?" I ask.

"Nouk, come home quick!" Jonathan's voice is frantic. "Charlie's had an accident; it's bad, Nouk. Meet me at Emory," he sobs. "He fell down the stairs. I forgot to lock the safety gate … He's critical."

I drop the phone.

* * *

CHAPTER SIXTEEN
ANOUK

April 11th, 2013
Morning

It was humid and overcast on the morning we bury Charlie. I stare numbly at the tiny wooden casket in the ground as rain pounds my umbrella, drowning out Reverend McCabe's prayer to the intimate crowd of close family and friends who have gathered. I look up to the angry sky. It's as though mother earth herself is grieving Charlie's loss. Jonathan rubs my arm as he holds me up. When Reverend McCabe has finished his prayer, he gives me a nod. It's time to say my goodbyes.

I kiss Charlie's teddy bear and throw it onto the casket. My motherly instinct beckons me to climb down into the hole and lie down in the dirt next to him. I may as well die too, now that my baby is gone. The pain is unbearable. I yearn to hold him in my arms again, to breathe in his baby smell, and to tell him one more time that Mommy loves him and Mommy is here.

Jonathan must sense my temptation because he tightens his grasp around my waist, pulling ever so slightly on my black chiffon blouse. Black really isn't a dark enough shade to represent how I feel. I keep replaying the image of Charlie's face when I saw him in Jonathan's arms at the hospital; Jonathan was weeping over him. Charlie appeared asleep, like he always does when he takes a nap. There were only a few drops of crimson on his otherwise untouched, perfect face. It was only a bump—a scratch. But when I kissed him on the cheek, it wasn't warm. I had arrived at the hospital twenty minutes too late. He had passed by the time I got there. I took him from Jonathan and cradled his body for what seemed like days, until Jonathan had to carry me wailing out of the hospital without him, but not before I cut a lock of Charlie's honey-blond hair.

I pull the lock of hair from my handbag and bring it up to my mouth in desperation. It's the only part of him I have to hold now. I hear Claire sniffle and sob behind me. For a brief moment, I feel like turning around and telling her to shut up, that her grief is *nothing* compared to mine. Brianna and Leanne meet my gaze and give me a sympathetic smile, but I can't return it. Reverend McCabe gives Jonathan an encouraging nod.

Jonathan clenches the blue baby blanket between his hands and brings it to his nose, deeply inhaling its smell before dropping it onto the casket. Now he is on his knees, in the dirt, sobbing next to my feet. I should find the strength in this moment to give Jonathan some words of comfort or reach down to stroke the back of his head, but I can't move. I'm frozen, selfish in my pity. Or maybe a part of me *is* angry with him. Angry that he didn't protect our boy—*my* boy.

Claire appears from behind me and pulls Jonathan off the ground into her arms.

"Shhh," she hushes, stroking his rain-soaked hair off his face.

"It's my fault," he says, wrapping his arms around her.

She pulls away from his embrace with urgency and grabs his face between her hands, forcing him to look at her. "It's not your fault, OK!" she says, shaking her head.

"I should have been watching him. I took a phone call. I should have watched him, Mom!" he sobs to her.

Claire pulls him close and wraps her arms around him. Ewan appears out of the rain and envelopes them both in an embrace. I drop my umbrella and just let the rain wash over me for a while, wishing it would wash me away with it while the groundskeeper shovels wet dirt over the casket until the teddy bear and the blue blanket disappear beneath the earth.

"Anouk," a familiar voice calls out behind me.

I turn around. It's Tom.

"I'm sorry, Anouk. I'm so sorry for your loss," he says, forlorn.

"I thought you … I thought you were in London," I mumble, wiping rain off my face.

"I cut it short. Jonathan called me," he says with a weak smile. He drops his umbrella to give me a hug.

I brace for the tightness of it. But it's different. There is a tenderness this time. I'm unsure if it's the scent of his cologne or the warmth of his hard body pressed against mine, but there is a strange sense of familiarity, and I feel safe wrapped in his arms. I hug him back hard and sob on his chest. He just holds me and lets me cry, occasionally wiping the rain off my forehead and offering me a tissue. We're both drenched, but I don't care, and he doesn't seem to care either. I'm lost in his embrace, and for a brief moment, I can forget the reality of where I am.

It's quiet. Nothing but the sound of the rain, the faint whispers of guests, and the smell of wet earth mixed with Tom's cologne.

"Tom, thanks for coming." Jonathan's voice brings me back to reality.

Tom releases his hold on me and shakes Jonathan's hand, placing his other hand on Jonathan's shoulder.

"I'm so sincerely sorry, Jonathan. I really am. Let me know if I can do anything for either of you," Tom says with a look of concern.

"We're having the wake back at our place. "We'd like it if you could make it," Jonathan says, trying to muster a smile.

"Of course. I'll be there," Tom nods to us.

Jonathan holds his muddied hand out to mine and puts his arm around my waist, kissing me on my temple as he walks me away to the car in silence. He opens the passenger door for me to get in, and as much as I try to hold it in, I can't. I slam the car door shut.

"Why, Jonathan?" I cry out, shoving his shoulder with my hand. "Why didn't you watch him! You should have protected him! Why? Why?" I ask, falling to the ground. "Why? I want to know," I howl, wrapping my arms around my stomach.

He leans down to hold me. "I'm sorry," he whispers in my ear. "I'm so sorry," he soothes, picking me up off the ground and placing me sobbing, wet, and dirty into the passenger seat.

When he gets into the car, he sits there, covered in mud, silent. A lone tear rolls down his cheek.

"I loved him too. I'll never forgive myself. You don't need to punish me, OK? I'll never forgive my-self for the rest of my life. Never," he moans, pulling at the steering wheel in anguish.

As much as I still want to be angry with him, I relent. The man is grieving too, and here I am, stick-ing the knife into an already open wound. I muster the strength to stroke his cheek with the back of my finger.

"We must find a way to heal together, Anouk," he sighs and starts the car.

I nod to him, too exhausted to speak.

* * *

Afternoon

Back at our house, Brianna greets us at the front door. Inside, the sweet scent of flowers fills the air.

"Honey, why don't you and Jonathan change out of your wet clothes before everyone arrives? The ladies and I will set up lunch. We've got it covered," she says, putting an arm around my shoulder.

Brianna really has been a blessing this past week, making dinners for Jonathan and me and leaving them at the front door. Leanne, Louise, and Kathy have been helping too and have made an array of cakes, sandwiches, and iced tea for the wake so that I didn't have to do anything.

"Thanks, Brianna," I reply with a weak smile.

Kathy, much to my surprise, has been a great support too. She offered to help me with the funeral arrangements given that Jonathan and Brianna were both in court, working. Kathy's brother-in-law, David, happens to be a funeral home director in town, and she drove me there to meet him.

I would have liked Jonathan to have taken me, to make decisions about the funeral service together, but he couldn't get out of work despite trying. Working has given him some respite from his grief.

I was an incoherent sobbing mess and could barely speak to David about the service proceedings when Kathy and I got there. I was grateful she was there, occasionally putting her arm around me and offering words of comfort as she spoke to David on my behalf. I was wrong about Kathy. She confessed in the car on the way to see David that she and Louise were starstruck when they'd met me for the first time at Brianna's. That explains why they were staring at me at Brianna's morning tea party.

Jonathan and I each take a shower and change before guests arrive to pay their respects. We greet them politely downstairs, but I can't bear to talk to anyone. I don't want to hear one more "I'm so sincerely sorry for your loss" or "my deepest condolences."

Reverend McCabe follows me into the kitchen with a cup of tea in one hand and a piece of cake in the other. Reverend McCabe has known the Fowlers for many years through the church, so when Ewan asked him to do the service, he willingly obliged.

"Anouk, you must find comfort and peace in the knowledge that Charlie is with his maker now," he says in his thick Scottish accent.

I feel a sob rise in my throat. Reverend McCabe's words don't make me feel better. *I'm* Charlie's maker, and he should be here with me, his mother.

Leanne interrupts. "Anouk, I want you to know that we're all here for you and Jonathan. If you need anything, just let me know, OK?" she says, giving me a hug.

"I appreciate you helping out today, Leanne."

I glance over at Jonathan, who's chatting quietly to Tony, Brianna, and Eric in the kitchen. He looks at me, disconcerted, before the chime of the doorbell interrupts.

"I'll get it," I mouth to Jonathan and go to open the door. It's Tom.

"Thanks for coming," I say ushering him inside. "I see you changed your clothes," I mumble. His round face looks forlorn.

"Yes," he says with a weak smile that is quick to disappear. He's looking down at his feet. He can't look me in the eye.

"You OK?" he whispers, his eyes now on mine.

I nod without a smile. "Come in. Have something to eat," I say, pointing toward the kitchen.

Ewan and Claire arrive soon after Tom, and they both embrace me at the front door without saying a word. Claire tears up, and I tear up again. They really are kind-hearted people, and I know that they are in just as much pain as I am.

Once everyone has arrived, Jonathan pulls me to his side in the kitchen. He taps his glass and says, "Folks, just gather around for a moment, please. I want to say a few words."

This is unexpected. I had no idea Jonathan was planning a speech. He continues.

"Anouk and I just want to thank you all for your condolences and supporting us at this difficult time. Your friendship means so much to us, and I have no doubt that we will be leaning on you at times ahead as Anouk and I come to terms with the loss of our Charlie. Life as we know it will never be the same. However, it's important that today we celebrate Charlie's life, although brief, and I want you to always remember him and the joy that he brought to us all. Charlie was truly a beautiful child. One of a kind . . ."

Jonathan's voices cracks and his eyes glaze over. He pauses to collect himself. I give him a reassuring nod as I feel a sob rise in my throat. I manage to hold it down and stay stoic for him in the moment so he can finish his speech.

He clears his throat and continues. "We must be grateful for the time we had with him. Thank you," he says, wiping his eyes. Ewan pats Jonathan on his back as he wipes a tear from his own eye.

I give Jonathan a kiss on the cheek, and we're approached by guests sharing stories about Charlie. It feels cathartic for a short while to listen to their personal memories. But it's been a while since I've seen Tom, so I wander through the house to look for him. I find him standing in a corner of the living room, flanked by Brianna and Louise. I pause to listen for a minute in the doorway. Tom appears uneasy, with his hands in his pockets, shifting his feet. He sees me standing in the doorway, and his almond-shaped blue eyes widen with relief as if he's pleased by my interruption. Then he gives me a pleading look, begging me to save him from the conversation, or perhaps he just wants to talk to me.

"Ladies, do you mind if I talk to Tom for a moment, please?" I interrupt.

They oblige politely and scurry out of the room rather quickly.

"I see you're popular," I quip, mustering a weak smile and taking a seat. He takes the seat opposite me.

"Good to see you smile, Nouk," he says, taking a sip of his iced tea. "Atlanta really is beautiful. I can see why you and Jonathan like it here so much,"

He gets up from his seat and paces across the living room, pausing occasionally to look at an ornament on display or take a sip of his tea. He really is quite striking. I can make out the outline of his athletic physique under his fitted black suit as he paces. It's easy to see why women would want to be around him.

He continues. "Speaking of Atlanta, I have about twenty orders for dresses for the annual Children's Charity Ball in June," he says, taking another sip of his tea.

"Actually, I'm on the ball committee, and I was going to ask if you could have Chloe and Alison design a dress for me. I'll be guided by your creative direction."

"Absolutely. What's the theme?" he asks.

"Under the Sea," I reply.

"Leave it with me, and I'll come back to you with a design," he says with a wink.

"Thanks."

"We miss you back in New York. When do you think you'll be back?" he asks with a hint of trepidation.

"I really can't think about that right now, Tom," I say with an exhausted sigh.

"Of course. I mean, there's no rush. I didn't mean that you need to rush back ... I actually quite enjoy being the CEO. It does have its advantages, you know," he says with a quiet chuckle.

"I can see that. The ladies clearly like you." I smirk. It feels good to have a laugh with Tom. He relaxes me.

"Anouk, I have to fly back to New York tonight. But there's something I've been meaning to say to you. Now that we're alone, there's something I must tell you, and I sincerely apologize for the inappropriate timing and for what I'm about to say, especially given you haven't gotten your memory back. But it has to be said now, face to face, as I don't know when I'll get to see you again." His voice is low and apprehensive.

"Go on," I nod impatiently.

"I need you to promise that you won't tell Jonathan, OK?" he says, running his hands down his face likes he's worried about my reaction to what he has to say.

"I don't keep anything from Jonathan," I say, somewhat annoyed and rising from my seat.

"Promise me ... Please. You'll understand why when I tell you what I'm about to say. It may come as a surprise, and Jonathan is also a good friend of mine; I don't want to hurt him, you, or your marriage by what I'm about to say," he says placing his hands on my shoulders. "Please promise me you won't tell Jonathan," he pleads.

"I promise, OK? Now tell me what it is. You may as well tell me now, Tom, as I couldn't possibly feel any worse than I do today."

His eyes look glassy, and his expression is serious. "Anouk, there could be a possibility that Charlie was … There is a possibility that Charlie was mine."

What?! "No. That's not possible!" I gasp, pushing his hands off my shoulders.

"Yes, it is Anouk. Remember how I told you that we went to London … That's where our affair started," he whispers.

What?! "No! No!" I wail, running out of the room.

"It's true, Anouk!" he calls out behind me.

I race upstairs to my bedroom and fall sobbing onto my bed.

***

CHAPTER SEVENTEEN

MIA

February 18th, 2011
London
Morning

"Anouk!" I call, knocking at her hotel door. "It's time to go. It's nearly eight! We're going to be late," I huff.

She was supposed to meet me in the lobby ten minutes ago. *Where is she?* I cup my ear and press it against the door. I hear muffled voices inside. *Who's with her?* I knock at the door again.

"Coming!" Anouk calls back impatiently. She opens the door ever so slightly, sticking her head out through the small gap. She's still in her robe, her hair is disheveled, and she has the smudged remnants of last night's makeup all over her face. Her eyes are glassy, and I can smell last night's alcohol on her breath. She was sober when I left her and Tom in the hotel bar at nine as I headed to bed. She'd promised me she was going to go to bed by ten-thirty.

"Are you hung over?" I ask her politely to hide my inner anger.

"I'm just running late," she mumbles, hand combing her hair into place. She can't look me in the eye.

"Really, Anouk." I sigh. "How could you get drunk the night before our fashion show!"

I've never really raised my voice to her before, but I've lost patience. Anouk's drinking has become worse over the past four months, and it's starting to impact her work. I've had to do all the fashion design for this season's collection because she says she's lost her creativity—not that she ever had any—and even our clients have started to notice that she's making mistakes with orders and she's moody. I feel like I'm her babysitter or worse, her mother protecting her from herself. It's *my* show, *my* designs, and I'm not having her compromise it.

"I'm fine," she says, waving her hand dismissively. "Just give me five minutes, OK?"

"Who's with you?" I ask, pushing on the door.

"Nobody ... Just give me five minutes, OK, Mia?" she says, trying to close the door.

"Who is it?" a male voice whispers to her behind the door.

I can't see who it is talking to her through the gap. She closes the door and whispers something to him, then she opens the door again. It's Tom.

"Morning, Mia," he gulps.

What is he doing here? Oh no. Of all men she had to cheat with, why did it have to be with Tom? My heart sinks in my chest. He looks picture-perfect, as always, not a hair out of place.

"I was just going through the final schedule for the catwalk models with Anouk," he says nonchalantly, buttoning up his shirt.

Anouk appears sheepish. I glare up at Tom as I feel a sob rise in my throat, but I manage to hold it down, and my shock and hurt are soon replaced with anger.

"Really, Tom?" I ask sarcastically, folding my arms.

Irrespective of my schoolgirl crush, I wouldn't have thought he would stoop so low as to sleep with her.

"I thought the three of us already discussed that in the bar last night," I retort.

"Yeah, well ... err ... I just had to check that Anouk remembered the finer details," he says coyly.

"Why doesn't it surprise me that she doesn't remember? Oh, that's right. It's because you both got drunk," I say.

Anouk rolls her eyes at me.

"You both have five ..." I pause to check my watch. "I mean four minutes to meet me in the hotel lobby. I'll hold the limousine. I don't want to be late, so I won't wait for you if you're late."

"OK, Mia. I won't be late," Anouk says before she shuts the door.

I hear them giggling like children as I walk away from the door toward the elevator. She doesn't care how much she hurts the people who love her. I feel the sob rise again in my throat, and I manage to hold it in. There's no one in the elevator, and I put my hands to my face and sob. She knows I care for Tom, and how dare she cheat on Jonathan? That man is so in love with her and would do anything for her. He would be devastated if he knew. I would give anything to have a husband like Jonathan. There's no surprise with Tom, though. Despite his reassurances to me otherwise over the years, he's only ever had eyes for Anouk. Even all my surgery and weight loss clearly weren't enough to turn Tom's head in my direction.

Tom and I have always been close friends, but I knew in my heart he was lying to me when I questioned his feelings for Anouk one day in the office. I wanted to believe otherwise, that perhaps I had a chance with him. He assured me he wasn't interested in married women. What a liar. I step out of the elevator into the lobby, and a wave of nausea washes over me. *Oh no*. I feel like I want to throw up.

* * *

CHAPTER EIGHTEEN
ANOUK

May 4th, 2013
Morning

Time is a well, and we fall into it grieving. Rather than providing words of comfort or emotional support to each other in the weeks following Charlie's death, Jonathan and I have all but stopped talking, selfish in our own pity. We are lost; a piece of who we once were is missing. We are broken, and we will never be repaired. The missing piece that bound us together, our Charlie, is gone.

It's a wonder how any marriage survives the loss of a child, and no doubt, many don't.

Jonathan has gone back to work; he intends to keep himself busy. For me, time has stopped altogether, and

I feel no purpose in getting out of bed. I have missed all my rehabilitation appointments. The thought of facing another day without Charlie is just too much for me to bear. Jonathan suggested I go back to work in New York a couple of days a week, and it's something I may consider, but I don't feel ready. Brianna and the ladies from the ball committee have been leaving baked dinners and cakes at my door.

"You must eat and get out of the house," Brianna groused at me yesterday when she popped over with some cupcakes.

I'm just not hungry, and I'm still reeling from Tom's bombshell at the wake. Just when I thought things couldn't possibly get any worse, Tom dropped *that* news on me. His timing with announcing the possibility that he could be Charlie's father couldn't have been more inappropriate; it's inconceivable. What the heck was he thinking? He had a sensitivity chip missing that day. Or he too was grieving in some strange kind of way. I guess if there is any truth to what he said, he would be grieving the loss of a son he never knew. And if Tom were lying—what would be his motivation? And why would I cheat on Jonathan? It just doesn't make sense. Besides, Charlie was the spitting image of Jonathan.

I hate keeping a secret from Jonathan, but now wouldn't be the time to tell him. That would be like pouring salt into an open wound, and I promised

Tom I wouldn't tell Jonathan. I hate myself for cheating on the man I love, and I hate myself even more for keeping a secret from him. I don't deserve him. How could I have betrayed him after everything he has done for me? The man I married and promised to be faithful to forever. *Darn*! I want to remember.

"Bye, Anouk. I'm off to the office," Jonathan hollers from downstairs as I lie in bed staring at the ceiling. A part of me wants to beg him not to go, not to leave me alone and instead to stay home with me, but I just don't have the energy for a fight.

"Bye," I murmur almost inaudibly and close my eyes.

***

Afternoon

I'm yelling at the car in front. "Nooo!" I wail, hitting the steering wheel with my fists. I accelerate hard. Oh no. I've lost traction …

The chime of the doorbell awakens me mid-nightmare. I check the time on my cell phone on the bedside table. It's 12:30 p.m. It's probably Brianna dropping by to check on me or hound me to go shopping with her. Or she's dropping off another freshly baked something that I don't feel like eating. I pull my robe on over my pajamas and hand comb my bed hair before I look through the peephole. It's Detective Mantle, and he's alone.

"Morning, Mrs. Fowler." He greets me with a sheepish look through the gap in the door.

"Err … morning," I rasp, tightening my robe before opening the door all the way.

"Look, I'm so sorry to drop in on you unannounced. I was wondering if I could come in to speak with you. I won't take up too much of your time," he says.

"Come in," I say through a suppressed yawn. "Um … I apologize for my appearance … I've just woken up. Been sleeping a lot lately." I sigh, rubbing my eyes.

"Mrs. Fowler, don't apologize. Err … I need your help," he says, looking around the foyer.

"Anouk, please. Call me Anouk … How can I help?" I ask impatiently, directing him to a seat.

"First, I'm so sincerely sorry for your loss," he says with a sympathetic look.

"Thanks," I murmur.

"I need to ask you some personal questions, if that's OK," he says softly, scratching at his head.

"Sure. Fire away." I shrug, apathetic.

"Where were you when your son fell down the stairs?" he asks, pulling out his notepad and pen as usual.

"I was in New York, meeting with a work colleague, Tom."

"So Jonathan was minding your son ... um ..." he stops mid-sentence to look at his notes.

"Charlie," I breathe. Tears well up in my eyes at the mention of his name.

"Thank you. So Jonathan was caring for Charlie while you were in New York. Is that correct?" he asks.

"Yes ... Why?" I ask, pulling a tissue from my robe pocket to dab my eyes.

"Oh, just protocol. I interviewed Jonathan at his office this morning about the events leading up to Charlie's fall and also at the hospital while you were flying back from New York. I just need to confirm with you that what Jonathan has told me matches your version of events. Can I take a look around?" he asks, rising from his seat.

"Sure."

He goes to the staircase and examines the stairs, taking notes. The baby safety gates are still in position at the top of the stairs. I'm not ready to put away Charlie's things or anything else that reminds me of him.

"He fell down the stairs, suffered a fatal head injury, and now my son is dead. What else is there to know," I snap at him, pointing at the staircase. The staircase I despise.

"The stairs were always impractical for a child of Charlie's age," I mutter. "You know Detective, it's ironic, isn't it? I was worried about the stairs from the day we moved in. I'll never forgive myself for moving in here," I say, heaving a sigh.

Detective Mantle pauses and puts away his notepad and pen. His brown eyes soften.

"You can't blame yourself," he says quietly, placing a hand on my arm. "Have you gotten any of your memory back?" He asks with a hint of trepidation.

"Nope," I say, raising an eyebrow.

"Was Jonathan an attentive father?"

"Yes. He adored Charlie," I huff in frustration.

"Do you trust Jonathan?" he asks.

"Yes."

"Do you have a happy marriage, Mrs. Fowler … err … I mean, Anouk?"

"Yes!" I snap. "And that's none of your business."

"Anouk, this is important. Is there anything, anything at all that you remember or can tell me that you think could help since we last spoke?" he asks, taking out his notepad again.

"Well, there is something," I mumble, putting my face in my hands in shame. "Detective, what I'm about to tell you is confidential, and I don't know if there is any truth in it … I can't remember … I don't want Jonathan to know because it could destroy my marriage," I plead. He closes the notepad and shifts his feet.

"I understand, Anouk. Go on." He nods. A ghost of a reassuring smile appears on his thin lips.

I take a deep breath. "Tom told me on the day of Charlie's funeral that I'd had an affair with him, and he thinks Charlie could've been his. I don't know why Tom would lie about such a thing. If only I could remember. Please don't tell Jonathan."

He looks at me, questioning. "I won't tell Jonathan ... but I do think that's something you should tell him."

"I will. In good time," I nod.

"Anouk, is there a possibility that Jonathan could have known about your affair with Tom and may have suspected that Charlie wasn't his? This could have given Jonathan a motive ..." he stops mid-sentence and bites his lip.

"A motive for what? What exactly are you saying, Detective?" I protest. "We're grieving, and I think your line of questioning is completely unwarranted given the circumstances—"

He interrupts me. "Has your marriage always been happy?" His tone is serious.

"Yes! Talk to our friends, my in-laws. Talk to Tom. He told me that Jonathan has always been in love with me."

"But you can't remember, can you, Anouk?" he suggests, raising an eyebrow.

"Are you implying that Jonathan killed Charlie?" I ask, standing up in front of him.

He recoils slightly at my reaction. "Anouk, what I'm saying is that I can't rule it out completely given what you've just told me," he says softly, waving his hand up and down in a soothing motion.

I take my seat, inhaling deeply. "Look, Detective, Jonathan would *never* hurt Charlie. OK?" I sigh. He nods, but I don't think he believes me, and I change the subject to direct it away from Jonathan.

"There *is* something else I need to tell you," I say rising from my seat to pace the room. "I think I may have wanted to hurt Mia," I blurt. "I'm not sure, but I had a dream today of the accident, and I was yelling at the car in front of me, and then I accelerated ... hard. It's all so confusing, but I think I actually wanted to hit her car," I cry.

He looks bewildered.

"Detective, I think I was trying to kill Mia."

* * *

CHAPTER NINETEEN

MIA

May 18th, 1996
Midnight

"How was it?" I ask her when she stumbles through the front door.

It's midnight. I decided to wait up for her because I couldn't get back to sleep. And I seemingly find myself living my life through hers these days as a way of escaping my nightmares; I hate how *he* can still torment me in my sleep.

She draws a sigh as she takes off a black stiletto, almost losing her balance in the process. She looks stunning in her black minidress as she sways down the hallway. Clearly, she's been drinking, and she's not happy. She flops onto the couch next to me.

"A total waste of time," she snarls as she kicks off the other stiletto.

"What happened?" I ask.

"The guy's a waiter, Mia," she huffs, rolling her eyes.

"So what?" I shrug. "I thought you said he was an actor," I remark, confused.

"Turns out he's been doing TV commercials part-time, which doesn't really count as being an actor. He's a waiter," she mutters.

"And … ?" I ask.

"AND he isn't a doctor, a lawyer, or someone going places," she pouts.

"But was he nice looking? Charming?" I ask.

"Yeah, he was … tall, dark, handsome. He paid the bill, and the conversation was … interesting, I guess, for someone not educated," she says sarcastically, rolling her eyes.

She pauses, momentarily reflective as she takes off her silver hoop earrings and throws them onto the coffee table. Perhaps she is having a change of heart about her date.

"Does it matter what he does for a living?" I ask, perplexed.

He sounds like someone I would date—that is, of course, if I had the chance or should be so lucky. Guys who like Anouk aren't interested in girls like me. I've never had a boyfriend. My father wouldn't allow it, and the only date I've ever had was when I was taken to the high school prom by a boy whose mother was an old friend of my mother's. He ended up kissing another girl on the dance floor in front of all the kids and took her home in his car. He just left me there, alone, and I had to walk home. I liked him; he was nice looking and polite. I wasn't crazy about him, but I was humiliated by the experience. I had already become accustomed to being labeled the fat girl and made fun of. But I cried for days after that prom, and the kids in town would not let me forget it either. It became too much to bear when they pointed and whispered from across the street on the odd occasion when I would go into town with my mother. I rarely went out after that.

But men are crazy about Anouk, and she knows it. She can have any man she wants.

"Mia, I'm not wasting time on someone who lacks ambition! I need someone who's as driven as I am, and I'm not settling for anything less. Besides, ever since I was a little girl, I dreamed of marrying a successful man. Someone with ... status," she says, playing with the lock of blonde hair draped over her shoulder.

Status. That word just rolls off her tongue. She makes no excuses for her snobbish arrogance. She never has in the short time I've known her. She really is so self-assured. I do admire that about her and wish

I could have her confidence, albeit without her arrogance.

"What about you, Miiiaaa?" she splutters, glassy-eyed. She's more wasted than I first thought.

"What about me?" I retort defensively, taking a sip of my cocoa.

"When are you going to get a man?" she laughs. It's a mocking laugh.

"I'm not interested right now," I lie sheepishly, shaking my head.

"Bullshit!" she retorts. She continues to laugh as she rises from her seat and goes to the refrigerator to pour herself some wine. I wonder if she knows how much she can hurt me sometimes with her words. I never let my hurt show—I wouldn't give her the satisfaction. She has a way of making me feel so small and inferior.

"Don't you want more for yourself, Mia? Don't you want the fairy tale, Mia? The perfect husband, the house with a picket fence ... kids?" she asks, taking a gulp of wine.

"Of course I do ... one day." I breathe a sigh. I've dreamed of that fairy tale since I was very young.

"Don't you often wonder how our lives will turn out, Mia?" she slurs as she sits down next to me. "We're a good team, you and me," she says, pointing a finger in my direction. "You're my best friend, and I want you to work for me."

Best friend? She's never said that to me before. I'm unsure if she means it or if it's the alcohol talking. We have become dependent on each other since meeting at design school, and she has become my closest friend. She's been good to me. Just as she can make me feel small at times, she also has a way of making me feel special, valued.

She continues. "I have a plan. With your gift for design and my business brains, we'll set up a fashion house like no other. Here in New York. Dad has finally agreed to give me the financial kickstart to get the business going," she slurs.

"Really? That's awesome!" I squeal with excitement.

"So, will you work for me?" she asks, taking another sip of wine.

"Of course I will." I smile at the thought. I've always dreamed of an opportunity like this.

"Good. Anyhow, back to your love life, or lack thereof," she giggles. She's mocking me again.

"Look, Anouk, you and I both know that men aren't interested in an overweight, acne-faced girl like me," I concede.

"I can change that, you know," she says straight-faced. Her voice is now serious. She sets her wine glass on the table and studies my face.

"I know a really good plastic surgeon. He could give you a new face and body," she slurs. "Where do you think I got these?" she says, cupping her breasts.

"I can't afford it, Anouk," She's already lent me more money than I can repay.

"I'll pay for it. Consider it an investment. I'll invest in you. If you're gonna be working for me, you need to look good. The fashion industry is full of beautiful people," she says, fluttering her eyelashes.

She really is a piece of work, and with that comment, she has made me feel small again.

"Get the surgery, Mia, and then you can get the man of your dreams," she giggles, taking another sip of wine.

"Do you want kids one day?" I ask her out of the blue in an attempt to change the subject.

"I don't have any desire really," she shrugs. "I wouldn't want to ruin my body." She laughs, running her hands up and down her sides. She's joking, but I know there's truth in it. She is the vainest person I know. "Not an appealing thought right now," she says, raising an eyebrow. "But if I did, I'd want a boy. Charlie. I'd call him Charlie … I've always liked that name."

"That's a nice name," I say. "I'd love to be a mom one day."

"You would make a great mother, Mia," she slurs, resting her head on my shoulder. This time, there's sincerity in her tone.

"Thanks."

She giggles. "We need to make you attractive to the opposite sex first. I'm gonna make an appointment for you with my surgeon," she teases, poking a finger into the rolls on my stomach through my pajamas. She really can be cutting, almost cruel.

Sometimes I resent her and really hate her. But I love her too.

* * *

CHAPTER TWENTY

ANOUK

June 22nd, 2013
Evening

I adjust my gold sari in the bathroom mirror reflection. Tom had Chloe and Alison design it, then he had it tailored to my measurements and delivered to my door. The inspiration for the dress was Tom's pet goldfish. He said he wanted me to wear something unique, and he thought that gold would stand out in the crowd.

Tom has been calling me for weeks since I last saw him, at the wake. I hadn't been returning his calls or emails, but I knew I would eventually have to take his call out of necessity for work. When I did answer the phone, he wanted to talk about the affair and Charlie's paternity. I told him that I didn't want to talk about it, and as far I was concerned, the "affair," as he called it, was over. I told him I was in love with my husband and that anything I had with him was in the past and never to be mentioned again; otherwise, we would never be friends. I said to him that it didn't matter now. Charlie was gone, and Jonathan and I were still grieving, and he needed to put the topic to rest for good. He reluctantly promised he would never speak of it again.

He wanted to know if I had seen the design he emailed me to wear to the ball, and I told him that I hadn't. I was too grief-stricken to even think about it.

"You're the CEO of Designite Fashion House, so I'm going to make sure you'll be the belle of the ball. Leave it to me," he said.

I think this was Tom's way of making amends. I would have worn whatever he chose for me, but this time, he was spot on; now that I'm wearing the dress, it looks amazing, and I love it.

"The limousine is here!" Jonathan calls from downstairs as I apply the last coat of gold shimmer to my lips and place a hairpin in my tight bun. My hair is quite long now so I can wear it up, and my scars stay well hidden.

"Did you grab the tickets and camera?" I ask Jonathan when I join him downstairs in the foyer. He looks dashing in his black tuxedo with his hair gelled straight back.

"Yes. Now, let's go. Mom and Dad will meet us there," he says, ushering me impatiently to the waiting limousine.

A gray-haired driver greets me outside. "Evening, ma'am," he says, opening the back door and lifting his cap.

"Wow, you look incredible," Jonathan whispers to me when he takes the seat next to me in the back of the limousine.

"So do you … I mean, you look handsome in your tux." I blush.

I feel awkward around Jonathan lately. It's been too long since we've spent time enjoying each other's company. He returns my smile and places his hand on mine, giving it a firm squeeze as he leans in to kiss me on the cheek.

"Let's have a good night," he says.

I nod to him and take a deep breath to calm my nerves as we drive away from the house. Jonathan has warned me that I might get unwanted attention tonight. He has tried to prepare me for the hounding media that may be there. Fortunately, my speech is so much better now. I want to have a good night with Jonathan, but I still feel empty. And I feel guilty about wanting to enjoy myself. I should be at home with my baby boy in my arms, putting him in his crib like I did at this time every night. I want tonight to be special, and I want Jonathan and I to laugh again. Lately,

I've felt lonely even in his company; he's been distant, and we haven't made love. I feel like we've lost our connection since we lost Charlie. It hasn't helped that Jonathan has thrown himself completely into his work, putting in long hours to cope with his grief. And I have been burdened with the guilt of not knowing if I cheated on him with Tom. I just can't bear to tell him, nor did I tell him about Detective Mantle's visit to our house last month and his line of questioning. I couldn't bear to see him in even more despair. The guilt has been tearing me apart, and I desperately want to reconnect with Jonathan. I miss us and the way we were.

When we arrive at the entrance to the Georgia Aquarium, I step out of the limousine to the sound of pop music and the excited chatter of a crowd that has gathered outside. It doesn't take long for a waiting photographer to recognize me.

"Anouk! Anouk! Can I get a photo?" he asks excitedly. "Together, please," he says, waving his hands and directing Jonathan to stand next to me. I give Jonathan a look of hesitation, and he gives me a reassuring nod.

"Sure," I say as the flash of the camera bulb goes off, momentarily blinding me. A few women huddled near the entrance are pointing and whispering at us. It's unnerving having all eyes on me.

"I think you're being recognized," Jonathan whispers in my ear.

"I'm nervous."

"Don't be. You can do this. Remember, just smile," he says and then winks.

All of Atlanta's elite have gathered, dressed in their finest. There are women dressed as mermaids and toned, muscular men dressed as Neptune, holding tridents. Those are the models for hire; they all have perfect, sculpted bodies and youthful good looks. Jonathan takes my hand and ushers me to the entrance, which is alight with the chatter of guests.

"Anouk!" a voice calls my name as soon as we walk inside.

It's Brianna. She's waving at me from across the foyer over the heads of the crowd. Leanne, Louise, Kathy, and their respective husbands are gathered near her. Jonathan and I give them a wave as Brianna moves through the crowd toward us.

"Hi, hon. So glad you made it," she says when she greets me, giving me a kiss on both cheeks in her usual over-the-top Brianna way. She looks stunning as always in my royal blue dress with the skew neckline; it hugs her petite frame perfectly. A pearl-encrusted halo headpiece sits atop her long, brown locks.

"You OK?" she asks, giving me hug.

I feel a sob rise to my throat. *No, I'm not OK; my son is dead, and I want him back.* But this is Brianna's night, and I want her to enjoy herself, so

I lie. "I'm fine," I say, waving my hand dismissively. "You look phenomenal in that dress," I praise in admiration.

"Thanks, hon … Hi, Jonathan," she gushes. "Come, I want you both to meet someone," she says, pulling me away from where our friends are standing.

I turn to Jonathan and roll my eyes at him apologetically. He follows as Brianna drags me past the queue of guests outside the ballroom doors waiting to be directed to their tables. After pulling me to the front of the queue, she stops in front of a plump older couple. The woman is dripping in diamonds, in particular, there is a large oval cut diamond necklace resting in her generous cleavage.

"Jonathan and Anouk Fowler, may I introduce you to Mayor Caldwell and his lovely wife, Anastasia," Brianna says formally.

"Lewis, please," the mayor says, holding out his hand in greeting.

"It's a pleasure to meet you both," Jonathan says.

"Anouk, it's *such* a pleasure to meet you!" Anastasia says in a southern drawl, shaking my hand with much enthusiasm. "I've been dyin' to meet you in person. Brianna told me that you live on her street. I just love your designs. In fact, I am wearing a Designite Fashion House dress tonight," she says, pointing to her corseted pale blue gown.

"Oh … thank you," I mumble, embarrassed.

I feel uncomfortable taking credit for something I didn't do. Chloe and Alison should be getting the accolades. Tom had said that Chloe and Alison received a dozen orders from Atlanta's elite women over the past few months for made-to-order designs for tonight's ball. They have been emailing me photos of the dresses they designed for tonight, but I only looked at a handful. I wanted Tom to see that I was showing an interest, but I haven't been able to muster the energy to even check all of my emails.

"Jonathan's a lawyer too," Brianna says to Mayor Caldwell.

"Ewan Fowler & Associates," Jonathan pipes in.

"Ah," he muses, looking at Jonathan over the top of his glasses. "You don't happen to be Ewan's boy, do you?" he queries, twisting his handlebar mustache.

"Yes, sir, I am."

"I've known your dad for years. He's a good man ... he told me you were taking over the business when I saw him not long ago in town. Give him my regards, will you?" he says, pushing his black frames up the bridge of his nose.

"He's coming tonight, so be sure to look out for him," Jonathan says, raising his voice to be heard over the music that has become louder.

"That's my cue, y'all. It's starting ... I need to find Eric," Brianna mutters. Eric and Brianna have seats at the Caldwell's table. "Being the ball organizer has its networking perks, you know, Anouk?" Brianna had recently quipped to me.

"See you inside later, hon," she chirps, giving us a wave before walking away.

The grand doors of the ballroom open, and the crowd is greeted by the same young men and women dressed as Neptunes and mermaids that we'd seen earlier. They are the waitstaff for the evening. After inviting the queue of guests in, they collect tickets and direct guests to their tables. Jonathan and I follow the Caldwells. A blonde mermaid takes our ticket at the door and directs us to our table in front of the stage. We wave to the Caldwells as they are directed to their table right behind ours. Inside, the lighting is in hues of aqua. Fishing nets and translucent paper lanterns in the shape of tentacled jellyfish hang from the ceiling. Each table is decorated with a trident candelabra, assorted seashells, and giant white coral in glass vases on sand-colored tablecloths. Jonathan and I are the first to take our seats at the table for ten. Brianna has organized the seating, but because I haven't seen much of her lately, I'm not sure who else is at our table, other than Ewan and Claire. A young man dressed as Neptune appears with Leanne and Tony following closely behind.

"I'm so thrilled we're at the same table," Leanne squeals when she sees me, taking the seat on my right. Tony greets us and takes the seat next to Jonathan.

"The guys can talk cars to their hearts' content," Leanne quips, giving me a hug. "You look amazing!" she yells in my ear over the eighties music blasting on the sound system. She puts an arm over my shoulder.

"So do you," I say.

Leanne looks youthful in her teal velvet Grecian dress. Her auburn hair is down, pulled off her face with a loose French braid to one side.

"It's a Designite Fashion House design," she says. "Tom gave me his contact details at the wake, and I haven't seen you for a while to show you. I've been worried about you." She frowns.

"I'm fine … really," I reassure her.

Tony and Jonathan are deep in car talk when Ewan and Claire arrive at our table with another couple I don't recognize. Claire introduces Rex and Jasmine Taylor to all of us at the table, and then Jonathan introduces me to Rex, who kisses the back of my hand in an old-fashioned manner.

"Pleasure to meet you, Anouk," Rex says. "I've heard all about you."

He appears just as charismatic as Ewan. Jasmine, on the other hand, greets us with a pleasant wave of her hand.

"Rex and Ewan have been best friends since they were little boys," Claire quips to the table, fluttering her false eyelashes at us. She gives me a wave with a forlorn look as she comes toward me. "Anouk, my dear. How are you?" she asks sincerely, giving me a kiss on the cheek with an embrace.

"I'm OK," I mumble.

"We'll catch up later," she says, patting me on the arm before walking over to give Jonathan a kiss on the cheek.

It's the first time I've seen Claire since Charlie's funeral. Jonathan told me that she had taken the news of Charlie's death extremely badly, and like myself, she was spending a lot of time in bed. I should have called her, but I've been so caught up in my own grief that I haven't been capable of thinking about hers. Ewan told Jonathan that she was taking prescribed pills to help her cope, saying that she'd found a new lease on life when Charlie came into her life, and then he was taken so abruptly. Ewan, however, has been a tower of strength for Claire, Jonathan, and me. Since he retired, he's been delivering healthy home-cooked meals to us whenever he can. Since Charlie passed, Jonathan has completely lost his passion for cooking, and I'm a terrible cook, so I'm grateful for Ewan's support.

"Hello, Lauren," Ewan says, rising from his seat. *Oh no. It's her.*

"Everyone, this is my daughter Lauren and her partner, James," Rex announces to the table.

Darn. She's at our table. Lauren and James give the table a wave and take seats on the other side. The music soon fades, and the high-pitched sound of a microphone turning on interrupts the chatter of the two hundred guests. I turn around to face the stage. It's Brianna and Mayor Caldwell.

"Good evening, ladies and gentlemen. My name is Brianna Sperling. I would like to welcome you to Atlanta's fifth annual children's charity ball. I want to thank you for being here. As you know, all monies raised tonight will go straight to terminally ill children and their families, so dig deep in your pockets, ladies and gentlemen. Tonight, we have a wonderful entertainment lineup, and after entrées, we'll be kicking off the silent auction. We also have a very special guest, ladies and gentlemen. Please join me in giving a warm welcome to our mayor, Lewis Caldwell." she says, handing the microphone to the mayor before she steps down from the stage.

"Thank you, Brianna. Ladies and gentlemen, please give a round of applause to our event organizer this evening, the wonderful Brianna Sperling," Mayor Caldwell says, pointing at Brianna as she leaves the stage.

Brianna blushes but appears to welcome the applause and attention, pausing on the steps to enjoy her moment in the spotlight. "Thank you," she mouths to the adoring crowd, taking a bow, before sashaying down the stage steps.

Mayor Caldwell delivers a quick speech to the audience before our prawn cocktail appetizer arrives.

I catch Lauren staring at Jonathan from across the table as he talks to Tony. Her eyes meet mine, and she gives me a smile that isn't in her eyes. She points to the tight, strapless aqua dress that's hugging her petite athletic figure. "It's one of yours," she mouths.

I nod to her. "Looks good on you," I mouth back.

I have to be polite. She is, after all, a paying customer. *Ugh!* She has thin lips and cold, dark eyes. Something about her makes me feel uneasy, but I can't put my finger on it. She gets up from her seat and walks toward me, then leans down and whispers in my ear.

"Anouk, I'm sincerely sorry for your loss of your little boy, Charlie. I really am."

But there is no sympathy in her voice and no warmth in her dark eyes.

"Thank you," I mutter, annoyed by her presence. She has no right to dare mention his name.

"Poor Jonathan has been working such long hours to cope with his grief," she whispers out of Jonathan's earshot.

What the? "Yes, he has. How do you know?" I ask, surprised.

"I work at Ewan Fowler & Associates now … didn't he tell you?" she gasps. Her mouth drops open.

"No, he didn't," I say, looking over at Jonathan, who has his back to us, still deep in conversation with Tony. *Why didn't Jonathan tell me?* I look back at

Lauren standing next to me, and if I didn't know better, I'd swear I could see a remnant of a smirk briefly cross her face.

"I'll catch you later, Anouk," Lauren says, walking back to her seat, but not before tapping Jonathan on the shoulder to make her presence known. He gives her a wave and continues talking to Tony.

Ugh! She is so *arrogant.* A live band starts on stage as dinner is served.

Leanne and I chat over our dinner of salmon on a bed of spinach, and before long, the guests at our table get up to dance. Brianna and Eric come out to the dance floor with us, and the ladies from the committee soon join us with their husbands. We form a circle and start being silly, taking turns in doing dance moves in the center. I laugh at Eric's attempt at breakdancing in his tuxedo. Jonathan takes my arm and twirls me around. He pulls me in toward his chest and whispers into my ear.

"You look ravishing tonight."

I relax in his arms and breathe in his cologne. I've missed this—having his body close to mine. After a few songs, we head back to the table. We've barely taken our seats when Eric, Tony, and James pull Jonathan away to take a look at the silent auction items.

"Back soon," Jonathan says, planting a kiss on my forehead.

"Anouk, there you are. I've been looking for you." A voice approaches. It's Anastasia. "You enjoying yourself?" she asks, taking a sip of her red wine.

"Yes. It's been a while since Jonathan and I have been out together."

"Really? I guess your work keeps you both busy?" Anastasia asks.

"Oh. Um, our son died not too long ago … I'd rather not talk about it … not tonight."

"Oh! I'm so sincerely sorry," she replies in surprise. "Would you like a drink?" she asks, lifting the champagne bottle out of the ice bucket.

"Yes, please," I say. I can feel my heart racing, and my breathing is rapid, like I'm about to have a panic attack. I want to go home.

Anastasia pours champagne into my glass as Claire returns from the dance floor.

"Claire," Anastasia greets her.

"Anastasia, so lovely to see you. It's been too long. I see you've met my daughter-in-law," Claire chirps. Claire appears to be in a rather upbeat mood tonight, more so than I had anticipated, and I wonder if it's the pills.

"Anastasia and I go way back," Claire says to me.

"We went to high school together," Anastasia declares in her southern drawl.

"Oh," I say with a fake smile, gulping my champagne.

"I didn't realize that Anouk Fowler was your daughter-in-law, Claire. I'm a huge fan," Anastasia says.

I'm starting to feel dizzy and nauseous. Either I've had way too much champagne, or the conversation has upset me.

"Ladies, can you please excuse me? I need to use the restroom." I swallow. *Ugh*! I feel ill.

I leave the table and hurry toward the restroom, where a queue of women has formed. When I get to a stall, I throw up quietly and immediately feel better. I clean myself up, apply some lipstick and perfume, and leave, taking a route on the opposite side of the ballroom to take a look at the silent auction items. A glass box with a one-carat Alexandrite silver ring catches my attention. It's exquisite. I read the description:

An exceptionally rare gem that will change color from bluish mossy green to red, depending on the light.

A hand taps me on the shoulder before I can finish reading the rest of the description.

"Evening, Anouk," says a familiar voice. It's Detective Mantle.

"Hello, Detective," I say, surprised.

"Beautiful, isn't it?" he says, looking at the ring.

"Yes, it is."

"Looking to place a bid, Anouk?" he asks, tilting his head.

He's finally calling me by my first name. "Oh no," I say, shaking my head. "Just browsing."

There's something different about him tonight. He appears more relaxed, but there is something else that I can't put my finger on.

"You look great," he says, looking at my dress.

"Thanks," I say, looking him up and down. "I almost didn't recognize you."

"It's amazing what a tuxedo can do." He smiles.

"No," I say, shaking my head. "Something's different." I study his face.

"I got a haircut," he says sheepishly, pointing to his head. "My wife said it was too long," he smirks.

His unruly salt and pepper hair is gone, replaced by a smoothly cut and styled mane. It makes him look much younger.

"Looks good," I nod.

"Um, my wife is here, and she would love to meet you. I think I mentioned that she's a fan of yours."

"Sure. Where is she?" I ask, looking behind him.

He points to the dance floor. "She's dancing up a storm with her friends … I don't dance," he says with a nervous laugh, shaking his head. He flashes a broad smile that I've never seen before.

"I have two left feet," he adds, rolling his eyes.

I laugh.

"How are you doing?" he asks with a concerned look.

"Good as can be expected," I shrug.

"Hey, I've been thinking about what you told me the last time we spoke," he says, taking a sip of his wine. "I know this isn't the time or the place, but I need to tell you something important." His tone is now serious.

His eyes dart around the ballroom. "Can we go outside?" he asks. "It's too loud in here with the music."

"Sure."

I follow him outside the doors, and he places his hand on my arm.

"Do you know if you have any enemies, Anouk? Do you know anyone who would want to hurt you?" he asks, seemingly out of the blue.

"No. Not that I know of or remember. Why?" I respond, shaking my head.

"I don't think you killed Mia," he blurts.

"How do you know?" I ask, startled.

"I had further testing done on what was left of your Corvette since we last spoke." He pauses to take in a deep breath. "Anouk, the brake lines had been cut. You wouldn't have been able to stop and might have hit Mia's car accidentally."

"What?" I gasp, holding my hand to my mouth.

"Look, I don't want to scare you, Anouk, but I'm concerned for your safety. Please be careful. Those brake lines were most likely cut deliberately," he whispers, scanning the area around us. He runs his hands down his face and takes another deep breath. "I think someone was trying to kill *you*."

What the? "Who?" I ask.

"I don't know. We found some DNA under the car—hair strands. We'll get those tested," he says, glancing behind himself again. "I'm sorry to tell you this tonight. Be careful, and call me if you remember anything, OK? I have to get back to my wife." He gives my hand a squeeze before turning to go back inside.

Oh no. Surely, he's wrong. It doesn't make sense at all. I feel a sudden tightness in my chest, and I'm finding it hard to breathe. I'm now truly scared. *Who would want to kill me?* I take in another deep breath and adjust my dress before going back inside to find Jonathan.

The music playing is loud, and I feel ill again. A wave of panic washes over me as I scan the room to locate Jonathan. I can't see him, and I weave my way through the crowd gathered near the silent auction items. I think I see him, the back of his head, but I'm not sure. He's talking to someone in the corner. When he turns his head in laughter, I can see his profile. It's him. He's talking to a woman, I think. I see long brown hair. Then he moves, and I can see her face. It's Brianna. *What are they talking about?* She whispers something into his ear, and he nods to her before she checks her watch, looks over to the stage, and says something to him before leaving.

I walk toward him, but before I can get close, he's intercepted by an amorous, stumbling Lauren. She appears to have had way too much to drink. *Ugh*! She takes his hand and walks him toward the dance floor. I follow and tap him on the shoulder to get him to turn around.

"There you are," he says, relieved, letting go of Lauren's grasp.

He's happy to see me.

"I've been looking for you," he says, planting a kiss on my cheek.

"I was in the restroom … feeling ill," I explain.

He takes my hand and walks me to the table. Lauren has quickly disappeared back to her seat next to James.

"I have a surprise for you," he says in my ear.

"Oh," I respond. "I've had a few of those tonight already." I frown. He's about to say something else, but the music suddenly stops, and he's interrupted by Brianna's voice coming over the microphone.

"Ladies and gentlemen, we're about to announce the silent auction winners, but before we do, I want to wish a special guest here this evenin' a happy birthday. Anouk Fowler, where are you?" she says, looking out to the crowd and holding a hand up to shield her eyes from the glare of the lights as she looks out from the stage.

Birthday? It's my birthday?!

"Surprise," Jonathan says, raising his eyebrows.

I nudge him, giving him a frown. *Oh no. This is embarrassing.* Jonathan lifts my hand up against my will so Brianna can spot us, and she points in my direction.

"There you are," she announces.

A spotlight appears on Jonathan and me. I blush in embarrassment, giving Brianna a dismissive wave. *Why didn't Jonathan tell me it was my birthday?*

"Anouk, my dear and talented friend, I want to wish you a very happy birthday from your husband, your friends, and me," she says, blowing me a kiss from the stage. *Great, all eyes are now on me.* "Now, let's get to the silent auction winners!" Brianna hollers into the microphone. I feel a sense of unease that all the guests have their eyes on me, and dread washes over me now that I know someone in the audience could maybe want to hurt me. I want to go home.

"Happy birthday," Jonathan says, holding his hands out wide.

"Why didn't you tell me it was my birthday, Jonathan?" I moan.

"Brianna and I wanted to surprise you," he says tilting his head. "What's wrong?" he asks before

Ewan and Claire rush over to wish me happy birthday with a hug.

"And the winner of the one-carat Alexandrite ring is Jonathan Fowler," Brianna announces. The room erupts with applause.

"You bought the ring?" I ask Jonathan, perplexed.

"Yes. A birthday present ... a precious gem for a precious gem," he smiles proudly. "Oh, and it also happens to be your birthstone."

"Jonathan, you shouldn't have," I gush. "I saw it on display ... I love it," I say, wrapping my arms around him.

"Excuse me, Anouk?" a male voice behind me interrupts.

I release Jonathan and turn around. It's one of the Neptune waiters.

"Yes," I respond.

He holds out his hand to shake mine. "Anouk, my name is Johann. You don't know me, but I know your friend, Mia.

He knew Mia? "Err, Johann, this is my husband, Jonathan." He shakes hands with Jonathan, wiping his wavy, shoulder-length brown hair off his pretty face. He looks barely twenty.

"Happy Birthday! Um, when I heard over the loudspeaker that you were here tonight, I thought I'd come and introduce myself. Mia always talked about you. I thought you may be able to give me her contact details. I lost touch with her a while ago, and I need to talk to her," he says.

Oh no. He doesn't know. I look up at Jonathan, and he nudges me to tell him.

"I'll leave you two to talk," Jonathan says. I give him a pleading look, but he wants me to be the bearer of the bad news. He gives me a reassuring nod.

"Nice to meet you, Johann," Jonathan says, shaking Johann's hand. "I'll meet you back at the table," he says, kissing me on the cheek.

"Err, um, Johann, I'm so sorry to be the one to have to tell you this, but Mia died a year ago in a car accident."

His pretty face drops. "Oh my god," he says, running his hand through his wavy hair in agitation. He's reflective for a moment. "What about her kid?" he asks me with a concerned look. I shake my head. "He wasn't in the car."

"He? So she had the baby?" he mumbles.

"I'm sorry, how did you know her?" I ask.

"Err, we met at a fashion show in New York … a few years ago. We had an on-again, off-again relationship. We would meet when I was on assignments in New York," he stumbles. His hazel eyes are glassy, and his hands are trembling. "The last time I spoke to her, she told me that she was pregnant … that the kid was mine. I told her I wasn't ready to be a father. I was twenty-one years old and told her I wasn't ready to settle down. I pleaded with her not to go ahead with the pregnancy, but she said she was determined to keep the baby. She said that because she was in her thirties, she felt it was her last chance to have a baby."

Oh my god, he's the father!

He continues, "We argued, and things got heated, and I told her that I never wanted to have anything to do with her or the baby, and that's the last time I spoke to her. I felt so guilty, and I called her a few weeks later to see how she was. I've never heard her so angry. She said to never contact her again ... Who's looking after the kid?" he asks.

"Mia's parents are raising him in Philadelphia."

He closes his eyes in anguish and shakes his head. "I really cared for her, Anouk. I just got scared ... I wasn't ready for that kind of responsibility, and I didn't want to move to New York permanently. I still live with my folks here in Atlanta," he says, forlorn.

I place my hand on his tanned, broad shoulder. "My friend Tom can get you her parents' details if you ever want to contact them to see your son," I say.

"No. I mean, thank you, but I think the kid is better off with his grandparents. I can't provide for him," he declares.

I should tell him what happened. I feel responsible for what happened to Mia.

"Johann, I was involved in the car accident that killed Mia. Our cars collided somehow, but I don't remember what happened, and I suffered a head injury in the accident. You might be able to help me ... I have questions about Mia. Can I get your phone number? If it's OK?" I plead.

He looks puzzled for a moment before giving me a smile and a nod.

"Sure," he says before scrawling his number on a napkin and handing it to me. "I'm sorry, Anouk, I have to get back to work. It was nice to meet you," he stammers before disappearing into the crowd.

* * *

CHAPTER TWENTY-ONE

ANOUK

June 23rd, 2013
Morning

"How do you want your eggs?" I ask Jonathan when he greets me in the kitchen.

"Sunny side up, please," he says, placing a kiss on my cheek before turning on the kettle. He looks terrible. His face has a gray pallor, the consequence of a hangover. We both drank too much last night. When we got home, Jonathan went straight to sleep. I was hoping for a romantic evening with him, to show him my gratitude for the ring, but he was out like a light the minute we got into bed. I guess I hadn't realized just how much alcohol he'd consumed.

"Have fun last night?" he asks, getting the instant coffee out of the cupboard.

Jonathan normally wouldn't be caught dead with instant coffee, but since Charlie's death, his gourmand tastes have disappeared.

"Yes. I love my ring. Thanks."

"How's the birthday girl?" he asks.

"Hungover." I yawn, adjusting my robe.

"Me too." He swallows. Last night's alcohol is back with a vengeance.

"You look terrible." I giggle as I crack the eggs over the frying pan.

"Thanks," he winces. "I have a headache. You look beautiful, even when you're hungover," he smirks. "Sleep well?" he asks as he gets two coffee mugs out of the cupboard.

"No. I didn't sleep well at all," I sigh. "In fact, I don't think I slept at all …"

I feel a sob rise to my throat and place my hand over my mouth to hold it in. *Hold it together, Anouk.* I repeat this mantra to myself. The strain of the past three months has become too much. I didn't dare ask him about why he didn't tell me that Lauren had started working with him last night. I didn't want to spoil the evening with an argument, especially after he bought me the ring. I have my back to him, and I don't want him to see me cry. Heaven knows how many times he has seen me cry lately.

He must have sensed my sadness, and he wraps his arms around my waist from behind. I feel the warmth of his breath on the back of my neck and can smell the remnants of last night's alcohol on him.

"I miss him too. We will get through this, Anouk. I promise," he whispers in my ear.

I nod and turn to kiss him on his lips. *Tell him, Anouk.*

"That's not why I couldn't sleep last night," I mumble. *Maybe now's not the time to ask him about Lauren.*

"What's wrong?" he asks as he continues to make our coffee.

I decide to refrain from asking about Lauren. I just don't want to fight about it, but I need to tell him what Detective Mantle told me. I'm scared.

"Last night … um … Last night, I saw Detective Mantle, and he told me that he doesn't think I killed Mia," I stammer, placing our breakfast on the kitchen table and taking a seat.

Jonathan puts the kettle down. "Well, of course you didn't. It was an accident," he says dismissively, getting the milk out of the fridge.

"No, I mean, he now thinks that someone may have been trying to kill *me*," I sob.

"What?!" Jonathan exclaims, then catching himself because he's carrying our coffee cups. "Who would want to kill *you*, Anouk?" he says in frustration.

"That's ridiculous," he scoffs as he sits down at the table, placing a hand on mine.

"Detective Mantle said the brake line of the Corvette was cut, Jonathan, and he thinks it was deliberate," I say, pulling a tissue from my robe to dab my eyes.

"Surely not," he says. "That's not possible." He shakes his head. "I had the Corvette serviced only a week before you had the accident, and the mechanic checked the brakes."

"Well, that's what he said, Jonathan," I retort.

"I'll talk to Detective Mantle, OK?" he says before taking a mouthful of eggs.

"I don't know how much more I can take, Jonathan. First Mia, then Charlie, and now someone's trying to kill me," I yelp.

He gets up from the table, takes a seat next to me, and holds me in his arms, stroking my hair.

"I don't feel safe, Jonathan. I want you to have a security system put into the house. I'm worried," I say sternly.

"If that will make you feel safer, I'll do it," he says, giving me a smile.

"Thanks,"

"Now, don't you worry. What are your plans for today?" he asks.

"Brianna asked me last night to join her for lunch at a café downtown. I don't know if I'll go. I don't feel great." I shrug.

"It might do you good to get out of the house. I'll drive you there, and you can call me when you want me to pick you up," he says.

"What are you going to do?" I ask, taking a sip of my coffee.

"Tony and Eric asked me last night to join them for a round of golf, so I might do that." He yawns as he takes our plates to the kitchen sink.

The home phone rings, and Jonathan answers.

"Hello? Yes ... Morning, Detective. We were just talking about you," he says, glancing at me and raising an eyebrow. "Enjoy the ball?" Jonathan asks him. Jonathan is silent for a moment and gives me a questioning look. "Yes, Anouk just told me. The suggestion is ridiculous, Detective. Why would anyone want to hurt Anouk ... Yes, I often drove it, and I had it serviced just before the accident. Oh, I can't recall where off the top of my head. I can give you the Corvette's log book ... What?! Why? Look, Detective, if it needs to be done to close this matter, I'll do it. I have nothing to hide. I'll come to the station tomorrow, and I'll bring the log book, OK? Goodbye."

He hangs up the phone and just stands at the kitchen counter, gazing out the window and running his hands through his hair like he always does when he's frustrated.

"What was that all about?" I ask.

"Detective Mantle wants me to give a DNA sample. They found DNA under the Corvette … hair … and he wants to rule me out as a suspect."

"Suspect?!" I gasp. *Oh my god. No.*

"My DNA will be all over that car … I often worked under it," he says. A worried frown appears on his forehead. I rarely see Jonathan looking worried. He takes a seat next to me at the table. "Anouk, I would never hurt you. You know that right?" he says, taking my hand in his.

"I know."

* * *

Afternoon

Jonathan gives me a ride into town to meet Brianna. Summer has arrived in Atlanta, and it's hot and muggy. Downtown is busy, with the cafés full of people enjoying the sunshine. I open the door to the French café where I'm meeting Brianna, relieved to be out of the heat. The decor is French provincial, and it's alive with the chatter of patrons and pop music.

"Hi, hon. You look terrible." She smiles when I join her at the table.

I feel immediately underdressed in my blue jeans, white shirt, and sneakers when I see Brianna. She's always immaculately dressed. Today, she's wearing a white Peter Pan-collared shirt and black capri pants with matching backless heels. She looks fresh, as always, and not like she had a late night at all. Her hair is up in a tight bun.

"Hungover?" she asks, handing me a menu.

"Yeah," I mumble. "I feel terrible." Last night's alcohol is rising in my throat. "You look well," I say as I take a seat opposite her.

"I only had a couple of glasses of champagne last night."

"So, how did it go?" I ask, enthused, as I look at the lunch menu.

"We're still counting, but I think we raised more money than last year," she says, clapping in excitement.

"That's fantastic, Brianna. Well done."

"Thanks, hon," she says, placing a lone strand of hair behind her ear. She waves to a middle-aged couple she recognizes as they enter the café.

"Is there anyone in Atlanta you don't know?" I ask sarcastically.

"No," she responds, serious. "I pretty much know almost everyone in this café." She smiles, pointing at people around the café and naming their names.

There's no doubt that Brianna is somewhat of an icon herself in Atlanta. Everyone seems to like her, and she is always invited to parties with some local celebrity or another.

"Did you have fun … on your birthday?" she asks.

"Yeah. I did."

"Like your ring that Jonathan bought?" she smirks.

"Love it."

"Good. Jonathan and I had been plannin' for some time to surprise you last night. He told me ages ago that the ball was on your birthday," she says with a smug look on her face.

A young waiter arrives at our table to take our order. We both order a pumpkin and feta salad and iced tea. I'm not that hungry today.

"Well, it certainly was a surprise." I sigh, handing the menu back to the waiter. I need to tell her everything, I can't keep it all inside any longer. Besides, I trust Brianna. She's been a good friend.

"You don't seem yourself today, hon. What's wrong?" she asks, taking a sip of water.

"I need to talk to you. I need your advice," I say, looking around the café. "I have so much I need to tell you, and I don't even know where to start."

She takes my hand in hers. "I have all afternoon to listen. I'm all ears," she says.

I start by telling her about Mia, her death, and how I can't remember the accident. I tell her that the police now think someone was trying to kill me, and that Jonathan may be a suspect. "The police want him to give them a DNA sample," I say.

"Jonathan, a suspect?" she scoffs. "He would never hurt you. He adores you, Anouk. Everyone knows that, honey," she says in her southern drawl. The waiter returns to our table with our salads. "Why would anyone want to hurt *you*?" she whispers so the waiter can't hear as he leaves.

"I don't know. I'm scared Brianna." My eyes dart around the café, studying the looks on the faces of the patrons around me. I'm feeling paranoid and unsafe, and my hands start to shake.

"Honey, no wonder you're so stressed. You should've told me all of this sooner," she says. "Don't worry, Anouk. Jonathan's a good lawyer; he'll know how to handle all of this," she says.

"There's more." I sigh. "You know my friend, Tom?" I ask.

She nods.

"The day of Charlie's funeral, he told me that we were having an affair before I had the car accident," I sob.

"What?!" Brianna asks me with a questioning look. "Is it true, Anouk?" she leans back in her seat and gives me a disapproving look. I can tell she's disgusted by the thought that I would have cheated on Jonathan.

"I don't know, Brianna. I can't remember," I sigh. "He thinks that Charlie could've been his. If what he's told me is true, then Charlie *could* have been his."

Brianna's eyes widen with shock. She puts down her knife and fork and leans forward in her seat. "Do you believe him?" she asks.

"I don't know what to believe anymore, Brianna. I just wish I could remember."

She rubs my hand.

"I just don't understand why he would lie about the affair. I mean, what would he have to gain by lying about it? He doesn't want Jonathan to know. He doesn't want to hurt him or destroy my marriage. I would never entertain the idea of cheating on Jonathan, Brianna."

"Have you told Jonathan?"

"No!"

"Who else knows about this?" she asks.

"You. Oh, and I told the detective who's been visiting me investigating the accident."

She frowns. "Why did you tell the detective?" she asks.

"I told him in a moment of despair, not long after Charlie passed."

"What did he say?"

"He started to question whether Jonathan could have known about the affair and then alluded to Jonathan having a potential motive to hurt Charlie. I dismissed it, of course."

"Jonathan would never hurt Charlie," she retorts, waving her hand dismissively.

"I know. I haven't told Jonathan what the detective said. I didn't want to upset him."

"What's the detective's name?" she asks suddenly.

"Detective Mantle."

"I know him. Well. He's a good man. Don't worry; I'll talk to him," she says. "But, Anouk, you need to tell Jonathan … about Tom."

"I don't want to lose my husband, Brianna. I love him. He's my life," I sob.

"You need to be honest with him. Tell him," she urges.

"I will. I just didn't want to hurt him, especially after Charlie." I pause for a moment, thinking. "Did you know that Lauren has started working for Jonathan?" I ask.

"Yes. Lauren told me. Why?"

"Jonathan didn't tell me. He's been distant in the past month or so."

"Look, you've both been grieving. Perhaps it slipped his mind."

"Do you think he's having an affair with her?"

"No way, Anouk. He is in love with *you*."

"Lauren had her eyes all over him last night."

"Maybe so, Anouk. But he only has eyes for you." She stops speaking for a moment and then slowly says, "Honey, Lauren is still holding a torch for him. She always has. He broke her heart, you know, when he broke off the relationship. She was devastated and didn't take no for an answer. She stalked him for a long while, and I told her many times to let it go."

What? How does Brianna know? "How do you know this, Brianna?" I ask, perplexed.

"Hon, I wasn't going to say anything because the past is the past, and I didn't want to make a fuss, but the truth is that I only put two and two together at our Thanksgiving lunch last year. I didn't recognize Jonathan at first when he arrived at our door. It wasn't until Lauren mentioned it at Thanksgiving lunch that I remembered him from years ago. Lauren introduced me to Jonathan back when they were dating and I was studying with Lauren at college. I only met him a couple of times."

What the?

"She was desperately in love with Jonathan, and her parents were hoping she would marry him. She probably persuaded Ewan to give her a job working with Jonathan, and Ewan would do anything for Rex."

"She needs to stay away from my husband. Something about her sends shivers up my spine. I don't trust her around Jonathan." I shudder at the thought of her and her cold eyes and thin, mean lips.

"Anouk, Lauren is my friend, an old friend, but she can be manipulative and unforgiving. She's used to getting her own way. Jonathan needs to watch out for her. Look, I don't want you to become paranoid, and I wasn't going to say anything ... I'm sure it's nothing to be concerned about, but she once told me in passing that when she jogs, she often goes past your house. And she said once that she stopped to take a peek in your window. I also saw her sitting in her car parked outside your house one day. She didn't see me drive past. It was on one of the days when I'm sure you were in New York."

Oh my god. "Brianna, it's her. She's the one who's been watching me!"

* * *

Jonathan arrives outside the café to pick me up. He parks the Volvo and steps out to open the passenger door for me.

"When were you going to tell me that Lauren was working for you?" I ask Jonathan, hiding my inner anger, when we're both in the car. I need to talk to him about it now given the news that Brianna has just given me.

"Didn't I tell you?" he frowns, shaking his head.

"No, Jonathan, you didn't," I say.

"Sorry. I thought I told you," he says as he starts the car. His shoulders drop, and he breathes a sigh. "I've been so preoccupied these past weeks. It must've slipped my mind," he says, scratching his head. He appears genuinely confused. "Well, if I didn't tell you, how'd you know?" he asks.

"Lauren told me, at the ball." My eyes narrow as I await his response.

"Oh. Well, to reassure you, it was Dad's idea. Dad asked her to work for him some time ago before he'd retired, and you know how Dad likes to appease Rex." He smiles, placing his hand on mine. "Why, are you jealous?" he chuckles, giving me a sheepish look.

"No, I'm not," I snap at him. I immediately feel guilty for being angry, especially since I haven't yet told him about Tom and me. I'm being hypocritical.

"Jonathan, I have evidence that it was Lauren who was watching me in the house. Us—watching us. Brianna told me today that Lauren has told her in passing that she jogs past our house. She told Brianna she looked in our window. It was *her* this whole time. I'm going to confront Lauren about it, Jonathan. She needs to stay away from our house!"

Jonathan looks shocked. "Look, it doesn't surprise me, Anouk, now that I think about it," he sighs, briefly releasing a hand from the steering wheel to run his hand down his face in frustration. He's talking to me, but his eyes are on the road.

"She's nosy. However, if you confront her, it's going to be awkward for me to work with her. You have no idea what she can be like, and she'll just deny it anyway. She'll go crying to Rex, then Rex will call Dad. I would prefer to keep the peace, Anouk. We have to work together, and I don't want Dad getting stressed about it. He's just made a full recovery. Besides, even though we think it's her, we can't prove it, and I don't think we should start a conflict between my parents and their friends based on hearsay," he says, his eyes now on mine as we stop at a light.

I turn in my seat to face him. "OK, but if she does it one more time, I swear, I'll confront her, whether you agree or not. Do you understand?" I frown.

"OK, I understand, Anouk."

* * *

CHAPTER TWENTY-TWO
DETECTIVE MANTLE

August 16th, 2013
Morning

"This is number twenty-three," the cab driver says, pointing to the modest red brick house. It's the home of Bob and Patricia Richardson, Mia's parents. Tom Avery gave me their phone number when I interviewed him a couple of weeks ago in New York. I arrived in Philadelphia on an early morning flight after I called and set a time to meet with them today.

I'm hoping the Richardsons can give me some insight into Mia and her relationship with Anouk. I don't have any other leads at this point. Anouk is not a reliable witness since she has no memory prior to the accident. Or so she says. But while I doubted her story at first, I now have a gut feeling that she's telling me the truth. Jonathan Fowler is my prime suspect. Is it just a coincidence that his child died and his wife's brake lines were cut? Did he try to kill his wife and the child after he discovered her affair with Tom? Did he suspect the child was Tom's?

I got suspicious that Jonathan is hiding something after his father, Ewan Fowler, called me shortly after I asked Jonathan to provide a DNA sample. Ewan was polite at first, making general conversation, and then he subtly started name dropping; making his political connections known before telling me that he wasn't happy I'd asked his son for a DNA sample, even though Jonathan was willing to provide one. I wasn't deterred by Ewan's protests.

It didn't take Tom long to confess to the affair when I interviewed him. He was adamant that Jonathan didn't know about his relationship with Anouk. "We were discreet. Jonathan's my friend," Tom said. Yeah, right. Some friend Tom is, sleeping with his friend's wife. I think Tom wants to maintain his friendship with Jonathan so that he can keep his job; he doesn't want to bite the hand that feeds him. But Tom could have had motive to kill Anouk, too. A jilted lover, perhaps? Tom said himself that it was Anouk who had broken off the relationship with him. Tom, however, was more than willing to provide me with a DNA sample and a legitimate alibi that checked out. He'd been out of the state on business for two weeks, starting before the car had been serviced and returning after the accident. He said, "I love Anouk. I always have, and I always will. I would never hurt her." But Tom was elusive when I asked him about Anouk's relationship with Mia. "It was complicated," he said. "They were good friends, dependent on each other almost. Each jealous of the other. They could be competitive at times, and they both had a fiery temper."

Jonathan's DNA was found, as expected, all over the Corvette. But "of course it was," he explained when I told him. "I drove it, cleaned it, and would often work underneath it," he said.

Lawyers always know what to say. But he's right. It's hardly admissible evidence to link to the cutting of the brake lines, given that he used the car. As it turned out, Jonathan's DNA didn't match the hair strands found caught on the car's frame near the brake line. The Corvette's log book, which Jonathan gave me, also checked out. It was legitimate. Jonathan had bought the car brand new. The brakes had been checked by a mechanic during a routine tune-up only a week before the accident, and the brake lines were in perfect working order at that time. The Corvette was only driven by Anouk and Jonathan, or so Jonathan tells me. He said he was working late the night of the incident, and then he headed home. And he was home when he got the call from the police notifying him of the accident.

This is the last roll of the dice in the investigation. There are no witnesses. If I can't crack this case soon, it'll go cold again. I'm determined to find the truth. For Anouk.

The Richardson's front yard is scattered with junk, rusting car parts, and gnomes. Lots of gnomes. The grass is overgrown, and there are two rusty pickup trucks in the driveway with their hoods up.

"Can you pick me up in an hour?" I ask the cab driver.

"Sure," he says, reaching for a card from underneath the visor. "How 'bout you call me when you want to be picked up. Here's my number," he says, handing me the card before I pay him and step out.

I can hear 1940s jazz music playing as I approach the house. The front door is open behind a broken fly screen. I hear the faint chatter of a couple talking and smell a stale cigarette stench coming from inside the house.

"Hello?" I call out.

A frail, gray-haired woman approaches the door. "Are you the detective?" she asks abruptly, without a smile.

"Yes. Good morning. I'm detective Kenneth Mantle from the Atlanta Police Department," I say, handing her my card through a hole in the fly screen.

She takes the card and puts her glasses on to read it. "Bob! Bob!" she calls inside from the door.

"What?" a gruff voice responds.

"That detective is here," she hollers to him.

"Coming!" His tone is impatient.

"I'm Patricia," she says, picking a cat up off the floor before opening the screen door.

She must be at least seventy years old, although it's hard to tell; the years seem to have been unkind to her. She's pale and underweight. Her collarbone is prominent under her baggy dress. She doesn't appear well.

"Come in, Detective. Take a seat. Bob won't be long," she says.

I notice her hands shake; she appears nervous. I follow her into the living room.

"Get off, you two!" she yells at two cats sitting on one of the maroon velour couches.

Her breathing is shallow, as though she's exhausted from yelling at the cats. The house is untidy and cluttered, full of photos and bric-a-brac. It reeks of cigarettes and cat litter; the smell is almost overpowering.

"Can I get you a water or a soda, Detective?" Patricia asks politely.

"No, I'm fine, thank you."

A bald, overweight man in a singlet and overalls appears in the living room with a beer in his hand. *It's too early to be drinking*. He appears a fair few years younger than her, maybe in his sixties.

"Hi, Detective. I'm Bob. I spoke to you on the phone," he says, reaching out his grease-covered hand to shake mine.

They both take a seat opposite me. "You have questions about Mia. So how can we help?" he says impatiently, looking at his watch.

"Yes. Look, I'm so sorry for your loss," I say.

Bob is expressionless and doesn't reply.

"Thank you," Patricia says quietly.

"Um, I need to ask you some questions about Mia, if that's OK?"

They nod.

"When was the last time you saw Mia?" I ask, taking my notepad and pen from my pocket.

"Geez, must've been six months before she died," Bob responds, scratching his head.

"Yeah, about six months," Patricia concurs.

"Look, Detective, we hadn't seen Mia much for years before she died. She left home when she was eighteen, and she rarely visited us after that," Patricia explains.

"And good riddance to her," Bob mutters under his breath, taking a sip of his beer.

"Bob!" Patricia scolds him.

"Well, it's true, Patricia ... She was selfish. She didn't appreciate what we did for her. Detective, she would only visit us if she wanted something—on the rare occasion," Bob says dryly, shaking his head in disgust.

"Detective, Mia was a troubled and difficult child at times. She lost both her parents when she was young. We adopted her when she was nine years old," Patricia says forlornly.

"You mean *you* adopted her, Patricia. I didn't want the kid," Bob snarls.

Patricia glares at him in disapproval. There is sadness in her eyes.

"We couldn't have children of our own. *I* couldn't have children," she murmurs stroking the cat next to her.

"Now, don't start getting all upset, Patricia. The detective doesn't need to hear all this," Bob snaps at her, shifting in his seat. He's agitated. I wouldn't dare talk to my wife so disrespectfully.

"Did Mia ever talk about her business partner, Anouk Fowler?" I ask, trying to change the tone of the conversation.

"Oh yeah, the high flyer in New York," Patricia says. "Anouk was a rich teenager, a spoiled brat according to Mia … but she was good to Mia. She let Mia stay with her in New York rent-free when they were studying, and Mia ended up working for her as a designer."

"And they became good friends?" I ask, looking at Bob.

"I never met the girl. Why is this relevant, Detective? Mia's dead," Bob sighs, looking at his watch.

"Well, as I mentioned to you on the phone, I'm investigating the car accident that killed Mia and injured Anouk. Anouk can't recall the accident and has serious memory loss. I need to know about their friendship given that they were both involved in the same accident and given that they worked together," I explain.

"Yes, they were good friends," Patricia says, giving Bob a disapproving look. She continues. "I met Anouk once when I visited Mia. She seemed like a snob; she was arrogant, but Mia was very grateful to Anouk for looking after her in New York and giving her a job. But in the past few years, their relationship had started to sour. In one of her more recent visits, Mia told me that Anouk was taking all the credit for Mia's designs. She felt that Anouk wasn't paying her enough for her work."

Patricia gets up from the couch and walks across the room to an undusted bookshelf.

"This is Mia, in her recent years," she says as she takes a framed photo off the shelf, wiping the glass of the frame with a finger.

She hands it to me. I look at the young woman in the photo. Bob seems disinterested in the conversation about his daughter; he's paying more attention to the cat on his lap.

"She's beautiful," I say.

"Was," Bob mutters, taking another sip of his beer. "Show the detective the other photo over there … before she had all that, whadda ya call it … plastic surgery," he says, pointing at a framed photo.

Patricia frowns at Bob and takes it off the shelf to hand it to me.

"Here, this is a photo of her when we adopted her," Patricia says with a smile.

It's the first smile I've seen from her since I arrived. She pauses, taking a finger and running it down the photo frame, remembering Mia fondly. A teardrop appears in the corner of her eye and rolls down her cheek. I study the photographs briefly. Mia as a child looks quite different from Mia as an adult. You wouldn't know that the photos were of the same person. She was much thinner as an adult, and her face had clearly changed; her facial features had become much finer. There are photos of a younger Mia and Patricia scattered around the room, but there aren't any of Bob with Mia.

"You know, she won a scholarship to design school. She was a bright child," Patricia says proudly. "We didn't have a lot of money, but we gave her what we could. I'm glad she got out of here, you know, made a good life for herself," she says, looking at Bob to gauge his reaction to the comment. He rolls his eyes in disapproval.

"I believe you're raising Mia's son, your grandson, is that correct?" I ask Patricia.

Bob checks his watch again and starts tapping a foot.

"Yes, he's at his father's for the weekend. The father couldn't handle the responsibility of raising the boy," Patricia says, picking a cat up off the floor.

"Not what we wanted at our age, Detective … looking after a little one," Bob says, annoyed.

"I understand," I say, looking around the room. The house is by no means child friendly or hygienic.

"Did Mia ever mention if she or Anouk had any enemies?" I ask.

"No. Mia never mentioned anything of the sort," Patricia says, shaking her head.

"Why?" Bob asks in his gruff voice.

"Just protocol," I shrug. "What happened with all her belongings in New Y—"

"We sold most of them. No room here for them, and the kid's father didn't want them," Bob interrupts before I can finish.

"I kept a box with a few of her personal items in the spare room," Patricia blurts out before biting her lip. She has said something she shouldn't have.

Bob glares at her, a cold stare, as though she has made an offer to me that she shouldn't have. He shifts in his seat and mutters something quietly under his breath, out of my earshot.

"I won't keep you much longer," I say to Bob. I can sense the tension between them and Bob's agitation, so I redirect the conversation. "I see you like cars," I say to Bob, pointing through the window at the pickups in the driveway.

"I'm a mechanic."

"Oh," I say.

It occurs to me that Bob would know how to cut someone's brakes. But what motive would he have to cut Anouk's brakes? He said himself that he never met her. His agitation, however, is making me even more curious about whether he's hiding something.

"You know, Bob, the brakes on Anouk's Corvette had been cut, causing her car to hit Mia's," I say matter-of-factly to gauge his reaction.

"What?" Patricia asks. Her mouth drops open in shock. She looks over at Bob with a questioning look.

"Patricia, get me another beer, would you?" Bob asks her through gritted teeth. She nods at Bob and scurries down the hallway to the kitchen with the cat trailing behind her. Bob gets up and walks toward me.

"You're barking up the wrong tree, Detective." His tone is threatening, and his face is close to mine. I can smell the alcohol on his breath.

"Maybe, Bob," I shrug. "But you have nothing to hide, do you, Bob?" My tone is even and unwavering.

His nostrils flare and he clenches his jaw. "You have a good day, Detective. I've got work to do. My wife will see you out." He takes a gulp of his beer. His eyes don't leave mine, and he maintains his stony-faced stare as he exits the room.

I can hear the quiet chatter of Bob and Patricia talking about something in the hallway. Bob's tone is angry. Patricia soon appears in the living room, and she's visibly upset about something he said.

"I'm sorry about Bob. He's just bitter she left us," she whispers.

"No need to apologize," I whisper to her with a reassuring smile. "Patricia, that box you mentioned that you had of Mia's belongings ... would you mind if I take a look at it?" I ask in a soft voice, careful not to upset her further. She shakes her head. She turns to look behind her, then looks out the window to check that we're alone.

"I don't mind. I'll just be a minute," she whispers and leaves the room.

She comes back a short time later holding a brown moving box. Her hands are shaking under its weight and she's breathless.

"Here, let me help you," I say, taking it from her. She holds it tight, hesitant to let go.

"May I?" I ask, and she finally lets go, staring at it blankly and biting a fingernail, deep in thought. "You OK, Patricia?" I ask.

She's now frantic, looking out the window to check on Bob's whereabouts. She touches me on the shoulder. "Take what you need, Detective, but hurry," she says, pointing at the box. "I'll be in the back yard helping my husband. Take all of it if you want, and see yourself out … Just hurry, before Bob comes back."

Her words are deliberate and carefully chosen, almost as if to serve as a warning.

"Detective, listen to me carefully." Her eyes are pleading. She has fear and desperation in her voice. "I'm dying," she breathes, her tone urgent. "I have terminal cancer, and I don't have long now, but I need you to know that I loved her, Detective. I made lots of mistakes. I didn't protect her like I should have, but I loved her like my own. I'm happy she got out of here. It breaks my heart that her life was cut short and that she didn't get to see her son grow up. She loved that boy so much. She was a good mother. A natural. Better than I ever was," she sobs.

"I'm sorry," I say putting a hand on her shoulder.

"I must go," she says, pulling her shoulder away.

"Thank you, Patricia," I call out as she disappears up the hallway.

I open the box. At first glance, it appears to be filled with old leather-bound books. I pull a couple of them out, but their covers aren't titled. I turn a few

of the pages, and it all becomes clear to me. Patricia
wants me to read them.

Mia's diaries.

* * *

CHAPTER TWENTY-THREE

ANOUK

August 17th, 2013
Evening

Jonathan reserved a table at one of the best fine dining restaurants in Atlanta. It's the first night we've been out together since the ball. He's still working long hours at the office, much to my dismay. I pleaded with him yesterday morning to cut down his hours, and he's assured me that he'll try. I don't like being in the house alone. Although he put in a home security alarm system, I don't feel safe when he's not there. He said he wanted to take me out for dinner tonight as a way of making amends for not being home much. I've been telling him for weeks that we need to talk, but he hasn't made the time, and I couldn't find any other good time to tell him about Tom.

I'm spending less time in bed moping, and I've started drawing, working out at the gym, and going out for lunch with Brianna and the ladies from the ball committee. I think about Charlie every day, and occasionally, after Jonathan leaves for work, I curl up on my bed and cry uncontrollably. Sometimes, I sit with the lock of Charlie's hair for a long time, smelling it and holding it against my chest, doing anything I can to feel close to him. I don't think I'll ever get over his loss. In recent weeks, Jonathan hasn't even mentioned his name and doesn't talk about him unless I do. It's become his way of coping, I guess.

"I'll show you to your table, sir," a young waiter says to Jonathan. The restaurant is hip, with contemporary, elegant decor. It's alive with the chatter of young and middle-aged patrons enjoying a Saturday night out on the town. Our waiter talks us through the chef's specials when we take our seat and then hands each of us a menu.

"Can we start with a bottle of your best house wine? Red, please," Jonathan asks him.

"Certainly, sir," the waiter replies. "I'll come back for your orders."

Jonathan's cell phone vibrates on the table, and I notice Lauren's name on the screen. *Urgh.*

"I have to take this," he says, rising from his seat. He covers the phone with a hand as he mouths at me, "I'll be five minutes."

I give him a disapproving look as he walks away from the table and goes outside to take the call. *What could she want?*

I watch him through the restaurant window as he stands outside on the sidewalk talking to her. He appears agitated, pacing back and forth. He sees me looking at him through the window and raises a hand in an apologetic manner. I nod to him and give him a smile. I don't want an argument tonight, and I need to trust him.

"Sorry," he says, kissing me on my forehead when he arrives back at the table. "That was important." He wipes sweat from his brow as he takes his seat. "I've been awaiting information about a case I'm working on. So, what did you want to talk about?" he asks, placing his hand on mine from across the table.

Tell him, Anouk! I stumble to get my words out, not because I can't speak; my speech is mostly fine these days. I just don't know how to tell him about Tom.

I'll start the conversation with the idea of me going back to work.

"Jonathan, I'm ready to go back to work a few days per week," I say, picking up the menu. "How do you feel about that?"

"Sweetheart, if you feel you're ready, I think you should do it. Annette said to you ages ago that it may help." He smiles.

Annette! That reminds me, I have an appointment to see her on Tuesday. I haven't seen her since I lost Charlie.

"I'm ready now."

"I'll support anything that you want to do, OK? You don't need my permission, Anouk," he says, browsing the menu. "Was that it?" he asks. "Was that what you wanted to talk about?"

"No, there's something else," I mumble.

The waiter interrupts with our wine.

"Have you decided, sir? Madam?"

Jonathan gives me a questioning look, awaiting my order.

"I'll have the duck confit please."

"I'll have the same," Jonathan says, handing the menu back to the waiter.

"So what else did you want to talk about?" he asks when the waiter leaves us alone.

I'm now pleased that I'm going to tell him in a crowded restaurant. I don't know how he's going to react to what I'm about to say.

"Jonathan, I'm sorry for what I'm about to say, and the truth is, I've been wanting to tell you this for a while, but with Charlie and …"

I gulp. *Just hurry up and tell him, Anouk.*

"Tom said I had an affair with him," I blurt. "I'm not sure if there's any truth in it; I can't remember, I promise," I plead.

I watch his face, awaiting a reaction. He's expressionless as he takes a gulp of wine. Maybe he's in shock. I want him to hurry up and say something. Anything.

"I'm sorry," I sigh, placing my hand on his.

He stares at his wine glass as he swirls the liquid in it, but he doesn't look at me.

"There's more," I say quietly. I cough to clear my throat. "Um, he said there could be a possibility, I'm not sure, but there is a possibility that Charlie was Tom's," I sob.

He stares blankly at me for a second or so and slumps back in his seat. I'm waiting for him to shout or get angry with me, but to my surprise, his eyes soften.

"That's not possible, Anouk. Charlie was *mine*. I'm sure of it. What does it matter now anyway, Anouk? He was *ours*, do you hear me?" He breathes a heavy sigh, leans forward in his seat, and places his hand on mine. "Charlie will always be our boy, and I won't hear another word otherwise. He was *our son*, OK?" he says quietly.

"Aren't you angry with me?" I ask.

"No. There's something I have to tell you too. I haven't been honest with you either," he says, playing with his wine glass again. "I already knew about the affair with Tom," he says, forlorn.

Oh no, it's true. "What?!" I say. My heart sinks in my chest, and I feel a sob rise in my throat.

"I've always known. After the accident, when the doctors told me that you'd lost your memory, I thought you wouldn't remember the affair with Tom. I didn't mention it because I thought you would forget about him for good and could fall in love with me again. You know, I was hoping it could be like it was before. Like it was when we first got married," he says, his voice heavy with nostalgia. "Tom doesn't know that I knew. One morning, I was out of my mind with jealousy. I told you I was planning to confront Tom, tell him that I knew, but you begged me not to. You assured me that you'd broken it off with him, that you wanted to make our marriage work. But you didn't want him to know that I knew and risk it impacting upon your business relationship with Tom, so you made me promise that I would never, ever say a word about it to him." He grimaces as if he's in pain or anguish from recalling the moment.

His eyes tighten, and his right hand clenches into a fist that he presses down on the table. I recoil slightly in my chair, my eyes darting around the restaurant, now worried he's about to make a scene.

"You have *no* idea how hard that was for me. To refrain from hurting him." he snarls, his nostrils flaring.

It's a look I've never seen before on Jonathan's face; rage—he's almost unrecognizable. Jonathan is usually so measured and even-tempered. But now, he's starting to scare me.

Thankfully his gaze begins to soften, and he slumps back in his chair.

"But I refrained, for *you*," he says in a low voice, leaning across the table to place his hand on mine. His eyes are glassy.

"The truth is I only told you Tom was gay so that you wouldn't think he was available once you recovered. I'm sorry. I just wanted you to love me again," he says with a quiver in his voice.

A tear appears in the corner of his eye. He runs his hands through his hair and slumps back in his seat again.

"I was selfish. I wanted you to myself, and I took advantage of the fact that you'd lost your memory."

"Jonathan, you should've told me. I've been carrying this burden around for so long. I'm sorry, too. I swear to you it will never happen again," I cry. "How did you find out I was having an affair with Tom?" I ask.

"Mia told me."

* * *

CHAPTER TWENTY-FOUR
MIA

March 3rd, 2011
New York
Morning

"Mia, please assure me that the design for the mayor's wife is going to be ready by Friday," Anouk orders when she storms into my office.

I put my work away under my desk and look up at her. She's glaring at me, eyebrows raised. She looks different today. She's wearing a black dress and a long cardigan over tights with a pair of knee-high boots. It's not the usual attire she wears in the office.

"I need to show it to her when I'm back from the Hamptons, Mia."

"Hamptons?" I ask her, perplexed, getting up from behind my desk.

Her eyes narrow. "Yes! Tom and I are leaving for the Hamptons today to do the photo shoot for next season's collection. Remember?" Her voice is impatient.

I look at her blankly. I have no idea what she's talking about.

"The photo shoot that Tom has organized," she huffs, placing her hand on her hip.

What? "Err … ," I say, scratching my head with my pen, trying to remember if he'd told me, but I don't recall Tom mentioning anything of the sort.

"Didn't he tell you?" She sighs, shaking her head in frustration.

"No. He didn't," I reply through gritted teeth, trying to hide my inner anger. *Why didn't he tell me this?*

"We'll be staying in the Hamptons overnight. I'll be back in the office on Monday,"

What? Nice of them to invite me. "OK," I say, hiding my disappointment. *They* are *my designs, after all.* "I was hoping to go on that photo shoot, Anouk," I say as the disappointment is revealed in my voice.

"Don't be ridiculous, Mia!" she snaps. "Someone needs to be here in the office, and I need you to finish that evening gown design. Please assure me you'll have it ready on Friday," she demands, glaring at me.

"Yes, of course. When have I ever let you down?" I say through a forced smile.

"Good. Let's keep it that way, and call me if you need anything," she retorts, flicking her blonde hair off her shoulder. A wave of nausea washes over me.

"You look terrible, Mia. Are you OK?" she asks, but there is no genuine concern in her voice.

"I'm fine, really," I reassure her. I'm lying. I do feel unwell this morning, like I'm coming down with the flu.

"See you Monday, then. Oh, there's so much to do before I leave. I need a coffee," she whines as she leaves my office.

I poke my tongue out at her back as she leaves and mimic her under my breath: "Oh, there's so much to do before I leave. I need a coffee." *Geez, she can be a prima donna.* I go to the restroom and walk back to my office via the kitchen so I can get a glass of water.

I see Anouk in the kitchen talking to Tom as I approach the doorway. He doesn't see me when he pulls her behind the door in an embrace. I hide behind a pillar and watch as he peeks out from behind the door to see if anyone in the office is coming, then kisses her urgently on the lips. My heart sinks, I can't catch my breath for a second or two, and a sob rises in my throat as I watch him kiss her so passionately and desperately. Why *her* and not me? But then, my hurt is replaced by anger.

Urgh! She's a piece of work, leaving me here to do all the design work while she and Tom live the high life together in the Hamptons!

My blood boils at the way she treats me and her husband. I can't let her get away with this. I know what I have to do.

I go back to my office, shut the door, and go to my desk. I pick up the phone and dial Jonathan's number.

He's quick to answer.

"Jonathan?"

"Speaking."

"It's Mia. Err … Listen, can I come over tonight? I need to tell you something … in private. It needs to be said in person."

There's brief silence at the other end of the line.

"I need to talk to you too. Why don't you come over at eight."

* * *

Evening

I arrive at Jonathan and Anouk's apartment with a bottle of red wine in hand. I know Jonathan enjoys a fine wine.

"Mia," he says in a welcoming voice when he opens the door. He greets me with a kiss on the cheek.

He smells good. "Please, come in," he says, ushering me inside. Something smells delicious in the kitchen. I'm now feeling quite hungry and remember that I haven't eaten much today. I'm feeling much better tonight than I did this morning.

I follow Jonathan down the hallway. Anouk and Jonathan's apartment is minimalistic, adorned with modern furnishings and abstract art. Not to my taste.

"Here, this is for you," I say, handing him the bottle of wine when we get to the kitchen.

"Oh, thanks. Good vintage," he remarks, looking at the label. "I've already opened a bottle of red. I'll save this one," he says with a broad smile. He places the bottle in a wine rack.

"What can I get you. Red or white?" he asks, running a hand through his hair.

He's still dressed in his work attire. His white shirt is undone at the collar, revealing a tanned chest.

"I don't drink. Just a glass of water, please."

I have never had a single drop of alcohol. Not even in my experimental early years—the legacy of growing up with an alcoholic father. I made a vow to myself at an early age that I would never drink, ever.

"Of course, I forgot. Anouk did mention to me that you don't drink. Good for you." He smiles. "I hope you're hungry. I've made a pot roast," he says, getting a glass from the cupboard.

"You didn't have to cook me dinner," I say. "I don't want to impose."

"I had to cook for myself anyway, and it was no trouble to cook a little extra," he shrugs, handing me a glass of water. He opens the oven to poke the meat with a fork. "That's another twenty minutes away," he says, closing the oven door.

"Anouk told me that you like to cook," I say, watching him maneuver around the kitchen with ease.

"I do. I find it relaxing," he says, pouring himself a glass of red. "Please, take a seat." He pulls a stool out from under the marbled kitchen counter. "So what did you want to talk about?" he asks, swirling his wine before taking a sip.

I'm starting to have second thoughts about telling him. He's the last person I want to hurt. Jonathan has always treated me well. I wouldn't say we're close friends, but we've been good acquaintances for years.

"Well ... why don't you go first. You said you had something to talk to me about."

"OK," he says, swirling the wine in his hand. "I don't know how to ask you this, but I guess there isn't any easy way, even though I'm not sure I want to know the answer," he says, wiping a drop of sweat from his brow. He starts running his hands through his hair nervously and takes a deep breath.

"Do you want me to go first?" I smirk.

"Yes, please," he says breathing a sigh of relief.

"Jonathan … Err … there's no easy way to tell you what I'm about to say either," I say. "But I think you have the right to know the truth, even if it does come between Anouk and me."

"Go on," he says. "I'm a big boy, Mia."

"Anouk and Tom are having an affair," I blurt.

His hazel eyes darken, and his jaw clenches.

"I knew it!" He picks up his wine glass and smashes it against a kitchen cupboard. "That bitch!" he yells, startling me.

"I'm sorry that I had to be the one to tell you," I say softly, trying to soothe him.

I've never seen Jonathan angry. It's scary. He is usually so controlled. He paces back and forth, breathing heavily and running his hands down his face, muttering to himself under his breath. I can't hear what he's saying. He inhales deeply, tidies his hair, and composes himself.

"I already had my suspicions," he sighs. "She's hardly home, she's been distant, and when she *is* home, she's always on her cell phone. That's what I was going to ask you tonight, if you thought they were having an affair, and you've answered my question. How long has it been going on?" he asks quietly, taking a seat. His hands are shaking.

"I'm not sure exactly, but they were getting pretty cozy in London," I confess. "You know they're in the Hamptons together right now."

"Yes, she told me she was going with Tom, and I trusted her, at least partly," he says shaking his head. "Did she tell you we've been trying for a baby?" he asks.

"No, she didn't," I say, surprised. "She said that you wanted kids, and she told me that she was considering it, for you," I empathize, placing my hand on his.

"Her heart hasn't been in it, Mia. Her mind is elsewhere, and now I know why."

Yes, because she's a selfish bitch who only cares about herself.

"I wanted to start a family with her. I *want* children. She says I'm pressuring her into having a baby. She thinks it'll ruin her career, but I'm not getting any younger," he says, forlorn.

"She's been saying the most awful, hurtful things to me when she drinks. And she's been moody. I honestly think she's fallen out of love with me, Mia."

He shrugs. I see the sadness in his eyes. He is so handsome. *She doesn't deserve such a perfect man.*

"I'm sorry. I know she loves you. She's told me many times." *But she loves herself more.*

"Yeah, right," he says, raising an eyebrow.

"Let me help you clean this up, OK?" I say, getting up to pick up the pieces of glass off the floor.

"Thanks … dinner should be ready shortly," he says, grabbing a cloth to wipe the red wine from the kitchen cupboards.

"Jonathan, please don't tell her I told you about her and Tom. I think it's best that she doesn't know you heard it from me."

"Of course. My lips are sealed. I promise," he says mustering a smile. He places a hand on my shoulder. "Neither of them needs to know that we know, OK?"

* * *

CHAPTER TWENTY-FIVE
ANOUK

August 18th, 2013
Morning

Jonathan lets out a faint groan next to me in bed when I kiss his cheek.

"Rise and shine," I whisper in his ear.

He slowly opens his eyes.

"Good morning," he says through a suppressed yawn.

"What time are you meeting Eric for golf?" I ask, hoping we can spend some more time in bed.

"Nine," he says, pulling my body close to his.

"You'd better get ready then; it's after eight," I pout.

"Oh, do you want some more lovin', Mrs. Fowler?" he chuckles.

"Maybe," I smirk and breathe a sigh of contentment. Last night we made love for the first time since we lost our baby boy. I feel like Jonathan and I have reconnected, especially now that we've been open and honest with each other. Not just reconnecting in a physical way, but I think we're getting our spark back. For the first time in a long while, I feel close to him. The pain of losing Charlie never leaves, but last night, I had some respite from my grief, if only for a fleeting moment.

"I'd better get going," he says, kissing me on the forehead before he gets out of bed.

"I'm going back to sleep," I say, blowing him a kiss. "I'll see you later."

I lie back down and close my eyes. When I wake up mid-morning, I go downstairs to make myself breakfast. The home phone rings.

"Anouk?" a familiar voice asks when I pick up.

"Yes?"

"It's Detective Mantle."

"Hi, Detective."

"I'm just checking in on you. How're you doing?" he asks.

"I'm OK," I say in an upbeat voice.

"Good to hear, Anouk. I've been worried about you."

"I'm fine, really, Detective."

"Listen, I went to the Richardson's house in Philadelphia. I met with Mia's adoptive parents."

"Oh, did you meet her son?" I ask.

"No. He was staying at his father's for the weekend. I want to question him. I'll need to get hold of his contact details from the Richardsons."

"No need. I have them. Detective, I met the father at the ball. A young man. He lives with his parents in Atlanta. That's odd, he didn't know of the child's whereabouts when I last spoke to him," I say, as I go to get his contact details out of my purse. I read the piece of paper that Johann gave me at the ball. "Johann Klomp is his full name." I give Detective Mantle his phone number.

"What did Mia's parents say?" I ask.

"Not much. Oh, I've got Mia's diaries. I haven't had a chance to read them all yet. I may be able to let you have a look too once I've gone through them. It may help you remember. Some of them go way back to the nineties."

"Thanks, Detective. I'd appreciate that."

"Listen, Tom's DNA results came back. They didn't match the hair strands found under the car."

"Detective, Tom is my friend. I've never doubted him. It's Lauren, Jonathan's ex-girlfriend, I now have suspicions about. And I have evidence. She's the one who's been stalking me," I huff. "I'm sure she wants me out of the picture."

* * *

CHAPTER TWENTY-SIX
DETECTIVE MANTLE

August 19th, 2013
Morning

I pull up outside Johann Klomp's neat two-story home in a middle-class suburb of Atlanta. I contacted him by telephone yesterday, and he agreed to meet with me.

"Hello, I'm Ada," A middle-aged woman with short blonde hair and flawless skin greets me at the door. "I'm Johann's mother." She smiles.

Ada is statuesque; tall and slender, with almond-shaped, translucent blue eyes, full lips, and high cheekbones.

"Morning, Ada. I'm Detective Mantle," I say, reaching my hand out to shake hers.

"Johann told me he was expecting you," she says with a smile. "I believe you want to ask him some questions about that Richardson girl."

"Yes, that's correct," I confirm.

"It's so sad. Johann was devastated to hear that she'd been killed in a car accident."

"Yes. It was sad. I won't take too much of his time."

"Johann," she calls out, "Detective Mantle is here. Please come in and take a seat, Detective. He won't be long," she says, directing me to the couch in the living room.

Above the mantelpiece of the fireplace hangs a painted portrait of Ada and many photos of Johann that appear to have been professionally taken. He is in different poses and locations. In one of them, he's shirtless. They look like the kind of photos you see in men's magazines.

Before long, an athletic-looking young man arrives in the living room, shirtless and dressed in sweat-pants. His hair is wet. It's hard to tell whether he's fresh from a shower or he's just been working out.

"Sorry to keep you waiting, Detective. I'm Johann," he says, holding out his hand to shake mine.

"I'll leave you two to talk. Can I get you a drink, Detective?" Ada asks.

"No thank you."

"Very well. I'll be in the kitchen if you need me," she says, patting her son on his shoulder before leaving the room. Johann takes a seat.

"So, Detective, you said on the phone you had some questions about Mia. How can I help?" Johann asks. His voice is calm and confident.

"How did you know Mia?" I ask.

"We met at a fashion show a few years back. We dated casually for a short time."

I pull my notepad and pen out of my pocket. He shifts nervously in his seat.

"Do you mind if I take some notes?" I ask.

He shakes his head. "I don't mind."

"What do you do for a living, Johann?" I ask with a smile. I want him to relax so he feels comfortable enough to talk.

"I'm a model," he says sheepishly. He rolls his eyes as if embarrassed.

"I see," I say, pointing to the photos of him on the catwalk above the mantelpiece.

He blushes and shrugs. "It pays well."

"How would you describe Mia Richardson?"

"She was a nice lady. She was generous," he says coolly. "I can't believe she's gone." He runs his hand down his forehead.

"What else can you tell me about her?"

He shrugs. "She was passionate about fashion design ... She took her job seriously. She was in-dependent, strong-minded. But she could be fragile emotionally."

"How so?" I ask.

"She told me that her childhood was difficult. She never wanted to talk about it with me, but I know she often had nightmares. She had difficulty sleeping when I would stay with her in New York."

"Can I ask why your relationship broke up?"

"It was just a fling. She had connections and gave me work," he says, blasé.

"So you were using her?" I frown.

"No, Detective. It wasn't like that," he says quietly. "She wanted more … a serious relationship. I was a fair few years younger than her, and I wasn't ready for a serious relationship. I mean, I live here with my parents. I'm trying to save money for my future, and I travel a lot for work. She lived in New York, and neither of us was willing to move. So the relationship ran its course," he says.

"Did she ever mention anything about her relationship with Anouk and Anouk's husband, Jonathan Fowler?"

"Not really. Oh, she did mention once that Anouk was difficult to work with at times. Demanding. She said that Anouk was good to her when they were young, that they were best friends, but Mia was tired of being underpaid. She felt Anouk was taking credit for her designs. That's about it, really. She never said anything about the husband." He shrugs.

"What was Mia's relationship with Tom?"

"She said they were good friends."

"Did she ever mention anything about Anouk's friendship with Tom?"

"She said they were close … Mia said to me once that she thought Tom was in love with Anouk." He shrugs. "Mia told me that she would get upset when Anouk would refer to Tom as her best friend. It hurt Mia to hear that."

"I believe you're the father of Mia's son. Is that correct?"

His broad shoulders droop, and he sighs. He looks over his shoulder.

"Detective, my mom doesn't know anything about this. My mom doesn't know I got Mia pregnant," he whispers. "Please don't say anything to my mom. It would upset her."

"But I thought you were caring for him on weekends here in Atlanta."

"No, Detective. I've never met my son," he says. There's sadness in his eyes.

What?!

"I broke up with Mia when she was pregnant. I told her that I wasn't ready to be a father. I couldn't do it. She was so angry with me. She said she would raise the child on her own. That was the last time I spoke to her." He runs his hands down his face in anguish.

"Johann, I visited Mia's parents recently, and they said the boy was staying with you here that weekend."

"No, Detective. The kid has never stayed here with me, ever," he shakes his head. "Mia's parents are raising him in Philadelphia."

* * *

CHAPTER TWENTY-SEVEN
DETECTIVE MANTLE

August 20th, 2013
Afternoon

I called Bob Richardson last night and told him I needed to ask him more questions about Mia. I could have asked him about the whereabouts of his grandson over the phone, but I want the element of surprise; I didn't tell him I was flying out to Philadelphia on a late afternoon flight today to pay him a visit. He said as far as he was concerned, Mia was dead so he had nothing further to say about her, and when I asked him if I could speak with Patricia, he said she was no longer living with him.

He said that since my last visit, her health had deteriorated quickly, and he'd had to check her into

Philadelphia's Temple University hospital. She was in palliative care, and she didn't have long to live. I made the decision to visit her before it was too late, and I'm concerned for her. I could turn up at Bob's house unannounced after I speak to Patricia. That's if she's well enough to talk. Time is of the essence, and I need to speak to her, especially now that she's on her deathbed and without Bob's intervention.

I've already read—skimmed—Mia's most recent and last diary entries. They were daily entries, mostly journaling her pregnancy in great detail. There were no details about Johann, and she didn't write after her baby was born. I assume that was because she didn't have the time anymore, as a full-time working mother.

On the flight to Philadelphia, I flick through an earlier diary from the nineties, which I randomly picked and placed in my carry-on luggage at the last minute before I left home.

I open it and read a diary excerpt dated June 17th, 1996:

When I was little, my mother used to tell me that a woman becomes invisible to men at a certain age.

Perhaps that's why she let him commit the acts that he did. She would become visible only then, once she'd served a purpose in his agenda, and she knew the secret would forever bind him to her.

For me, age is irrelevant. I've always felt invisible, except when he was home.

And I feel it now as I walk through the city and as I wait to order my usual coffee in the same coffee shop on Fifth. I'm the girl you don't glance back at over your shoulder.

But I won't be ignored. No.

Just you wait; I'll demand your attention.

You'll see me.

I promise ...

And I'll be beautiful. Transformed, like a butterfly when it emerges anew from the cocoon.

And then I will be wanted. Desired. Loved.

* * *

Evening

By the time I arrive at the hospital, it's starting to get dark. A gift shop in the foyer is closing for the night. I ask the shop assistant if he has any flowers just before he closes the doors. He hands me one of the last two bunches of sunflower bouquets. He says because he's already closed the till, he'll just give them to me. He refuses payment, and I thank him profusely. I'm not in uniform, but people never cease to surprise me. In my line of work, I often see the ugly side of human behavior, horrific crime scenes, and it's the little things, like an unexpected generosity, that stop me from losing faith in the human race and remind me of the good in the world. That, and the sanctuary of coming home to my loving and understanding wife each day after a long shift like this one is going to be. I'm lucky to have her. I'd give her anything; I want her to be happy.

But the one thing she desires above all else, I can't seem to give to her—a baby.

The doctors confirmed it's not her, it's me, and potentially not helped by the stress of my job. They say it *is* possible; we just have to be patient and keep trying.

The hospital is relatively quiet. I approach the older woman at the hospital reception desk and hold up my badge. "I'm here to visit a patient, Patricia Richardson."

"Evening. Let me check for you." She types on her computer keyboard. "Is she expecting you?" she asks with a furrowed brow.

"No." I shake my head.

"She's in palliative care. She may not be well enough to talk to you, Detective."

I nod to acknowledge that.

"She's in room ninety-seven. Go to the end of the hall and take the elevator."

"Thanks."

I can see Patricia lying there, asleep, through the window as I approach the door. Tubes are coming out of her nose, and she's been hooked up to a drip. She's gaunt and gray looking.

Silently, I walk into her room, close the door, and place the sunflowers in an empty vase on her bedside table. But despite my attempts at being quiet, my presence awakens her. She opens her eyes slowly; they're dull and sunken.

"Detective," she whispers in a raspy voice. The hint of a smile appears on her face.

"Patricia. I brought flowers," I say quietly, taking the seat beside her bed.

"Thank you," she mouths.

"Can I get you anything?" I soothe.

She shakes her head. She lifts her hand up and I take it in mine. She feels cool and bony.

She winces. "I need to tell you something," she coughs as she tries to sit upright.

"Rest, Patricia," I say, adjusting her pillow.

"I must repent. Bob can rot in hell. He hasn't visited me once," she wheezes. "I was a terrible mother to Mia," she whispers. She lets out a faint groan. "Bob . . ."

"Take your time, Patricia." I pat her hand.

"Bob ... abused her," she rasps. "I didn't do enough to stop it." She squeezes my hand.

Oh no. It's true. Mia alluded to that in her diary.

A tear rolls down her cheek. "I didn't protect her from him. I was older than Bob. I was weak, I didn't want to lose him. I didn't want to be alone," she stutters. After catching her breath, she continues. "I loved her. I should have protected her." She sobs quietly.

I don't know what to say to Patricia. And I can't say I'm sorry; she is just as guilty as Bob is for not reporting it.

"Where's Mia's son, Patricia?"

She's wheezing again. Her mouth is moving, but there are no words.

"The father—" she coughs.

"The father has him?" I interrupt.

She nods slowly, taking a shallow breath.

"But I spoke to him. He said he's never met the boy and that his son is with you and Bob," I say softly.

"No, Detective, he's lying," she rasps, shaking her head.

What?!

"Bob made a deal with him against my wishes," she stammers.

Deal?

"I wanted to raise him myself, Detective. Bob ... that bastard. Make Bob pay, Detective," she whispers.

"What was the deal, Patricia?" I ask softly.

Patricia coughs and wheezes. She starts to gasp. A young nurse comes into the room and gives me a disapproving look.

"She needs rest," the nurse huffs.

"Yes, I was just about to leave. Thank you, Patricia," I say, pulling her blanket up under her chin.

My cell phone rings. It's Detective Stevens.

"Ken, you need to come back to Atlanta on the next flight." His voice is urgent. "There's been an incident at the Fowler house."

* * *

CHAPTER TWENTY-EIGHT
ANOUK

August 20th, 2013
Afternoon

It's a hot and humid afternoon, and Emory's main reception is particularly crowded and noisy. The sound of crying babies echoes through the foyer. Their cries are distressing, and I can't help but think of my Charlie. I feel a tightness in my chest as I wait in the long queue to see the receptionist. I'm late for my appointment. When it's my turn, the receptionist directs me to go straight to Annette's office; she's expecting me.

"Anouk, it's so good to see you!" Annette exclaims when I arrive at her office door. She appears youthful today. Her long hair has been cut to shoulder length.

"Come in. Excuse my mess, Anouk. I've been extremely busy this week." She sighs as she frantically tidies up the paperwork that's cluttering her desk. "Please, take a seat," she says before sitting down at her desk. "How have you been?" she asks, pulling a file out of the desk drawer.

"I'm doing OK, I guess. All things considered," I mutter.

"You missed a lot of appointments," she grouses. "What happened?"

I stare at her for a moment as I prepare myself for what I'm about to say. I don't want to cry. I don't want to remember. I take a deep breath.

"My son died."

Annette is expressionless for a brief moment, then a sympathetic frown appears on her face. "I know," she says placing a hand on my arm. "Anouk, I am deeply sorry for your loss. I really am."

"How did you know?" I ask.

"It's in your medical records," she says, pointing to the file on her desk.

"My medical records? But I haven't seen you since he died," I say, confused.

"Yes, you have, Anouk. I saw you after you lost your son. Don't you recall?"

"Annette, I haven't seen you since April," I say, scratching my head.

"I know. Anouk, I wonder if you've had more memory loss since I last saw you," she says, flicking through her paperwork.

"My memory since the accident is perfectly fine."

She tilts her head to one side and studies my face. I don't think she believes me. "Have you had any memories come back to you from before the accident?"

"No."

"Your speech is better." She smiles as she flicks through her notes. "And nightmares? … Are you still having those?" she asks.

"I haven't had one for a while now. Annette, I'm positive I haven't seen you since my son died. I know it."

"Anouk, I've seen you since you had the car accident. I first saw you as my patient on the nineteenth of October last year. Here, it's in your file notes," she says, pointing to the file.

She hands it over to me. I scan the date on the page. I do remember clearly seeing her in October last year. I scan through the file, and the last date I saw Annette according to her notes was the morning of the fourth of April. The morning before the day Charlie died.

"Annette, my son died on the fifth of April … this year. I haven't visited you since that date. My son died the day after I last saw you," I say, handing the file back to her.

A sob rises in my throat. The thought of Charlie makes me cry. I hold my chest.

"What?" she says, taking the file from me with urgency. She frantically flicks through the notes.

"Anouk, I'm so sorry that you don't remember … Your son died in the car accident last year," she says softly.

"No!" I gasp. "My son died from a fatal fall at home."

Annette's eyes widen in shock. "Here," she says hesitantly, pointing to a hospital medical record from June two thousand twelve as she hands me the file.

"What are you telling me, Annette?" I ask.

"Your baby died in the car accident," she stammers.

"How is that possible. It doesn't make any sense!"

My eyes scan the page of my medical file, and the notes confirm what she's saying.

"My son died on the fifth of April!" I raise my voice at her. "Ask my husband."

Annette recoils, startled by my outburst. All color drains from her face, and she tilts her head quizzically. Then she leans forward in her seat, placing her elbows on her desk.

"Anouk, you lost a baby, a boy, at twenty weeks gestation, in the car accident," she says quietly. Her eyes are searching mine for answers. "Oh my god, Anouk. I'm sorry. I thought you knew." She sighs, placing her hand on her forehead.

"No! No!" I sob into my hands.

Annette's face is distorted in anguish. She gets up from her desk and puts an arm around my shoulder.

"You're wrong," I say, holding my chest. I can't catch my breath.

"Take a deep breath, Anouk. Do you want me to call your husband to pick you up?" she asks, passing me a tissue.

"No. I'll catch a cab home," I say, snatching the tissue from her hand. "I have to go. I need to speak to my husband."

* * *

Afternoon

I quietly sob in the back of the cab on the way home from Emory Hospital. Oh my god. I lost a baby at twenty weeks; Charlie's brother. Why would Jonathan keep such a secret from me? I call Jonathan's cell phone, frantic. It goes straight to his voicemail, so I leave a message.

"It's me. Meet me at home as soon as you can ... We need to talk," I say in a calm voice, hiding my anger.

I want to hear the truth from Jonathan. The thought of losing two children is just too much to bear. I wrap my arms around my stomach in anguish, lay my head back on the headrest, and close my eyes.

My cell phone vibrates. It's Brianna. "Hello," I whisper.

"Hi, hon. How are you?" she asks in an upbeat voice.

"Not good," I sniffle.

"Honey, tell me what's wrong," she says softly.

"I lost a baby," I cry.

There's a moment of silence on the end of the line. "I'm so sorry, Anouk. I know you miss Charlie so much."

"No, I mean I lost a baby in the car accident, Brianna. I just found out at Emory. It's in my medical records," I cry into the phone, not caring if the driver can hear my conversation.

"Didn't Jonathan tell you this?"

"No. I mean, maybe he did when it happened, but I can't remember. I don't know what to believe anymore, Brianna. I'm so confused."

"Oh, Anouk."

"Jonathan has lied to me so many times, Brianna. I don't know if I can trust him anymore."

"Where are you?" she demands.

"I'm on my way home from Emory, in a cab."

"Honey, I'm comin' over tonight. I'm worried about you," she sighs.

"I just need to go home to talk to Jonathan … I can't believe that bastard never told me!"

The middle-aged cab driver glances at me wide-eyed in his rearview mirror, wondering what the hell is going on.

"Now, now. You wait for his side of the story first, OK? Maybe he did tell you and you forgot. Maybe you didn't both know at the time that you were pregnant again. It is possible you weren't showing. You're so petite," she says softly.

"But why hasn't he talked about it since I've recovered? It doesn't make sense."

"Honey, maybe it's too upsetting for him to talk about. You've both been through so much. Maybe it's just too painful for him to ever mention. He doesn't want to suffer any more hurt. He nearly lost you too in that accident, Anouk. He's been through a lot."

"I'm not so sure what to believe anymore."

"He loves you, and he wouldn't ever hurt you. I'm sure he was protecting you from the truth," Brianna reassures.

"I'm not far from home. I'll call you tomorrow, OK?"

"OK, hon. I'm always here for you if you want to talk to me, OK? Call me anytime."

"Thanks, Brianna. I'll speak to you later," I say before ending the call.

"This driveway, please," I say to the cab driver.

When he turns in, I see that Jonathan's not home yet. *Darn!* The Volvo's not parked outside, so he must be working late again. Anxiety ripples through every nerve of my body, and I start to shiver. The cab driver notices my hand shaking when I pay him.

"Ma'am, are you all right?" he asks, taking my cash.

"Yes, I'm fine. Thanks," I lie before I get out of the cab to go inside.

* * *

Evening

I take a cool shower, throw on a pair of shorts and a T-shirt, and go downstairs to start dinner in an attempt to calm my anxiety and redirect my thoughts, anything to take my mind off the grief. It's a balmy night, so I decide to make a chicken salad. I can't stop shaking. I feel an overwhelming sense of dread at the thought that Jonathan has lied to me once again. I don't know if I can forgive him this time. I'm overwhelmed with anger at the thought of the possibility. I hear the front door unlock as I'm chopping the chicken. I take a breath to compose myself as his footsteps get louder as he approaches the kitchen from the hall. *Stay calm, Anouk.* I reflect back on Brianna's advice. I need to get his side of the story and try not to become irrational.

"Hi, sweetheart," he says, placing his briefcase on the kitchen counter. He walks over to me and kisses me on the cheek. I smell alcohol on his breath.

I don't look at him. "Hi." My voice is flat.

"How was your day?" he asks, placing a hand on my arm.

"Not good," I mumble.

He's standing beside me, but I can't look him in the eye. I keep chopping.

"I saw Annette today," I say. *Just say it, Anouk.* "She told me I lost a baby in the car accident ... I was twenty weeks pregnant with a boy," I say matter-of-factly. I feel his body flinch. "Did you know about that?" I ask calmly.

"Anouk, can you look at me? Please stop chopping and look at me," he says, placing his hand on mine.

"Did you know that?"

"Please look at me," he pleads.

I put the knife down and turn toward him, glaring, and he gives me a nervous smile. I search his eyes for the answer. For the truth. But I can't read them. He grimaces, closing his eyes.

"Well?" I ask impatiently, placing my hand on my hip.

"It's true," he says in a quiet voice. His eyes are glassy.

"Oh my god," I gasp, placing my hand over my mouth. "Why didn't you tell me?" I ask, banging my fist on the kitchen counter. *Ouch*.

His shoulders drop. "I did what I thought was best for you at the time," he says in a soft voice. "You were in the hospital, fighting for your life, and when you woke up and couldn't remember me or our life together ... I made a decision, right or wrong, that it was best you didn't know. There were times when I wanted to tell you, but I just couldn't bring myself to. I was grieving too. I didn't want you to suffer more. I didn't want *us* to suffer."

"No. No!" I wail. "It's not fair. Why us." I punch at his chest. "You lied to me so many times!"

He turns his back on me to get a glass out of the cupboard and pours himself a scotch. He takes a gulp of the liquor and turns back to face me. He's reflective for a moment.

"I did it because I love you. I was protecting *you*!"

I recoil. "Protecting *me*?" I scoff. "And it's your fault we lost Charlie. You were minding him. You should have protected him! You probably lied about that, too!"

"Enough, Anouk!" His eyes darken.

"How do I know that you didn't hurt him out of jealousy? You thought he was Tom's baby, didn't you?"

"Don't be ridiculous," he says, taking the last gulp of his scotch. He slams the glass down on the sink.

"It's true, isn't it, Jonathan? You haven't even mentioned his name since he died! Charlie. His name was Charlie. Say his name … Go on, say it!" I scream at him. "It's your fault he's dead. I'll never forgive you. Ever!" I wrap my arms around my stomach in the agony of my grief.

"That's not true. I loved him too. Stop it, Anouk. Enough!"

"You killed him. You killed my Charlie!" I push my hands into his chest.

Then it happens. It happens so fast, before I register what's happening. In a flash, his hands are around my neck, and he's pushing my back against the kitchen counter. It hurts. I want to scream, but I can't find my voice. The full weight of his body is on mine.

"Charlie," he says. "There, I said his name," he snarls. "He wasn't even *yours*," he whispers cruelly in my ear through gritted teeth. His grip around my neck tightens.

What did he just say? I feel light-headed, dizzy. I can't breathe; I'm gasping for air, and I can't move. My eyes plead with his, but I don't recognize the eyes looking back at me.

His fingers tighten further around my throat. My head is spinning, and I can't see his face. I muster the strength to reach up and grab his hands, but they slide off, slick from our sweat. He releases his grasp and I inhale sharply, gulping in a deep breath.

"Wha—" I can't catch my breath.

"You selfish bitch!" he spits. "I was a fool to take you back after your affair with Tom. Everything I did, I did for *you*!" he says, poking a finger on my chest.

"What do you mean he wasn't mine?" I stumble backward against the counter, off balance, holding my neck.

"He was Mia's and my son," he says, deadpan, as though it meant nothing, before he turns his back to me to go pour himself another scotch.

* * *

CHAPTER TWENTY-NINE
MIA

March 3rd, 2011
New York
Midnight

"Ha ha!" Jonathan lets out a hearty chuckle, revealing the most beautiful smile. A dimple appears on one cheek. I gaze at his face and wonder if he has any idea how attractive he is. I can't take my eyes off him.

"Where did you learn to tell jokes like that?" he asks, taking another sip of his wine.

"My father used to tell them to me. Well, actually, he wasn't my father by any stretch of the imagination. I was adopted." *Don't think about him, Mia.* I shudder at the memory of him. *Don't think about it, Mia!* I repeat this mantra to myself, but the smells and sounds still permeate my senses—there is no escaping *that* memory. *The combined stench of body odor and diesel on his overalls mixed with his vile, alcohol-laden breath. The filthy acts committed by his grease-covered hands. The pathetic whining sound of her voice begging him to leave me alone, time and time again ...*

"Oh. I'm sorry," he says with a frown. "I never knew that about you," he says, raising an eyebrow.

"Yeah, well, I don't tell too many people." I sigh. "If you met my adoptive parents, you'd know why."

"Tell me, how did you end up being adopted?" he asks with a questioning look.

I take a deep breath.

"Only if you're comfortable talking about it, of course," he says.

"It's fine," I nod. "Well, err ... my real parents were killed in a car accident when I was young. I was staying at my grandmother's house at the time; she continued to care for me when my folks died, but she died too not long after. I didn't have any other family members, so I ended up in foster care for a couple of years, shuttled around to quite a few different families. Very few couples want to adopt a plump seven-year-old." I shrug. "They all want a baby. I was adopted at nine by an older couple who couldn't have kids."

"Can you remember your birth parents?" he asks.

"Yeah, I remember them well. My dad was a doctor. I was a daddy's girl—when I saw him, that is. He was often on call, so he was rarely home. And when he was home, it was either too late in the evening and I was asleep, or he'd come home after a shift at the hospital, while I was at school. He was the center of my universe. I remember crying every time he left the house because I knew I wouldn't see him for a day or two. That feels like weeks when you're a kid. I was an only child, and I remember spending a lot of time with my mother, watching her sew. My mother was vivacious, full of life, and my father adored her. I'll never forget the way he looked at her. He was very much in love with her." I smile. "She was a seamstress."

"That explains why you're so talented at what you do," he says.

I blush at the compliment.

He breathes a sigh and gives me warm smile. "How about I open that bottle of wine that you gave me?" he says, getting up from the dining table. He stumbles on his way to the kitchen. He's already finished a bottle by himself.

"You sure you won't join me with some wine?" he calls out from the kitchen.

"No thanks," I call back with a chuckle.

"So, Mia, tell me, how come a woman as beautiful as you doesn't have a boyfriend?" he slurs as walks back into the dining room with the bottle of red.

I laugh, "I'm not lucky in love." I blush.

"I don't believe you. You could have your pick of men," he says as he opens the wine and fills his glass.

"You'd be surprised," I say through a nervous laugh. "No one has ever said that to *me* before." I flush, embarrassed.

"It's true, Mia. You're beautiful. Stunning, in fact," he says, leaning forward in his seat.

Oh my. He oozes charisma. It's hard not to find him attractive. It could be so easy to fall under his spell; he's alluring without even trying, I could easily just lean in to kiss him right now. The thought crosses my mind as he studies my eyes awaiting my reaction to his comment, but I can't do it; he's married to my business partner, my friend. I shake my head at the thought and come to my senses.

"I think you've had too much to drink and it's impairing your judgment," I say, waving my hand at him dismissively. I can't believe he just said that to me. I'm flattered, but I now feel uncomfortable, awkward. "Thank you," I say, taking a sip of my water.

"How on earth do you put up with so much shit from my wife?" he asks out of the blue. "She doesn't appreciate how hard you work for her," he says, shaking his head.

"Jonathan, she's been good to me over the years, so that's why I put up with it. I know she appreciates what I do for her. She just doesn't show it at times." I shrug.

"You know, I've told her that she should pay you more. You're worth a lot more," he says before taking a gulp of wine.

"I did ask her for a pay raise when she made me partner. She said she would give me one, but I still haven't received it," I sigh.

He's right, I am worth more money. I've just never pushed the topic with Anouk because, after all, she did pay for my plastic surgery bills over the years. To the best of my knowledge, Jonathan is not aware of that, and I'm not going to confess it to him right now. I'm too embarrassed to admit it.

"Mia, without you, that company wouldn't be where it is today, and Anouk knows it. Make sure you get what you're worth. Do you hear me?" he says, placing his hand on mine.

I nod to him. I'm taken aback by his sudden concern for my well-being.

"Your designs are amazing. You're a talented woman," he says, pointing a finger at me from across the table.

"So, you're not going to tell her that you know … that you know she's seeing Tom?" I try to confirm and redirect the conversation away from me.

"No. I'm not going to tell her I know—for now. I think she'll come to her senses. That's what I'm hoping will happen."

"Aren't you angry?" I ask, confused.

"Of course I'm angry," he says, forlorn. "But it is what it is, Mia," he says, shrugging. "I can't make someone love me. She has to do it of her own free will."

Oh my. I could love you. What is Anouk thinking? If you were my husband, I would never leave home.

"You're a good man, Jonathan. She's lucky to have you," I say, taking his hand in mine. "It's late, I really have to go." I pick my purse up off the table and rise from my seat.

He takes my hand between his and gives it a gentle squeeze.

"You don't have to, you know," he says suddenly.

I sit back down. *What? Is he saying what I think he's saying?*

"Pardon me?" I mumble.

"You heard me," he says softly. "You don't have to go. Why don't you stay with me tonight?"

He gets up from the table and walks behind me. *What is he doing?*

He places a hand on my shoulder, and with the other hand, he gently slides my long hair to one side of my neck. *Oh no.* Ever so tenderly, he kisses the nape of my neck. *I can't do this. I want to but I shouldn't.* He shifts his body beside mine, towering over me in my seat. He places a long finger under my chin, forcing me to look up at him. He studies my eyes momentarily to gauge my reaction, and before I can react or process the moment, his lips are on mine. I freeze, only for a second or two, from the surprise. But then it's too late. He's got me. I'm under his spell, and I kiss him back. It feels so natural, so right, and yet so wrong. *Oh no, what have I just done?*

He pulls his lips away, but his face is close to mine.

"Please stay," he pleads as he combs my hair off my face with his hand. "Stay with me tonight," he whispers.

"OK, I'll stay."

* * *

CHAPTER THIRTY

ANOUK

August 20th, 2013
Atlanta
Evening

I feel disconnected from my body. I can't compute what he's just said; that Charlie was Jonathan's child with Mia! *It can't be true. Charlie was mine.*

"No, Jonathan!" I cry out. I feel nauseated.

He turns to me. "There, I finally said it," he slurs.

I glare at him with pure hatred.

"It's the truth. Don't start acting like you're the victim here. You weren't exactly the loving wife," he says with a snigger. "It's all your fault; it never would've happened with Mia had you been faithful."

He glares at me, glassy-eyed, with disdain. I don't recognize the man I once loved looking back at me. I study the look on his face and jolt. The hint of a memory flashes through my mind, and then I really remember:

A hazy image of a black car wrapped around a lamppost, steam pouring from its engine. The sight of Jonathan getting out of its passenger side door. It's blurry through the rain pouring onto the windshield, but I see him. He doesn't know that I can see him, standing motionless on the road in the dark. Oh no. My baby! I remember the cramping, stabbing pain, the feeling of grief, his tiny body losing life inside me, and the rage I feel at the betrayal when he glances in my direction for a brief moment before turning away and running into the darkness …

"You *snake*," I rage. "You were there that night," I say, trying to catch my breath. "And you left me there for dead."

"What are you talking about?" he mutters, waving his hand dismissively.

"You were there that night. I remember you getting out of that black car. Mia's car. You left us both for dead! You could've saved our baby," I yelp, falling to the ground in the corner of the kitchen.

My head is spinning. I wrap my arms around my waist.

He walks toward me, silent, coolly taking a sip of his scotch. I can't tell if he's angry, but I hold my hands over my head in readiness for a blow.

"It wasn't like that," he says in a low voice, standing over me.

His voice is calm now, measured almost, but I'm too scared to look up at him.

"I don't believe you."

He slams his glass on the counter. He kneels next to me as I sob with my face in my hands.

I shudder. I don't know exactly what triggered it in this moment, whether it's his breath on my neck or it's something we've said, but I now remember why I was there that night. I bolt upright, standing over him. He stands up as well, his face close to mine.

"I remember. You were with Mia that night, in her car. I saw her kissing you in the car. I remember it now so clearly. I followed her car after work to see if *you* were having an affair with her. I had seen the texts on your cell phone that morning, that you were planning to meet her that night!"

He shakes his head, bewildered. "I was breaking it off with her," he slurs, running his hands through his hair.

"I saw you look in my direction. You recognized the Corvette; you must have known it was me in the car, pregnant with your son! You left us. *Both* of us … Why?" I cry out.

He closes his eyes and rubs his forehead.

"I left to get help, and then it occurred to me that it could have been your Corvette," he says, quickly opening his eyes. His demeanor changes, and he has a look on his face that I've never seen before. It's a look of panic. He starts pacing back and forth across the kitchen in an agitated manner.

And then I realize that I've put myself in danger. Now that he knows I know, I'm scared of what he might do. His eyes are wild and unreadable.

"I went over to your car to check. I saw it was you, and you were barely conscious, barely alive when I got there. I was calling your name, comforting you through the window. I couldn't get to you; you were trapped. Our cell phones were damaged, so I *had* to leave to find help. I didn't want to leave you," he says. "You have to believe me. It's the truth!" he says, fast and breathless.

"I heard the sirens approaching, I knew they would be able to help you. I was in shock, and I ran. I didn't want you to know I was with her that night. I didn't want her to come between us, so I caught a cab back to my office to pick up my car and then headed home. When I got there, I got the call from the police telling me you'd been in an accident. I promise, I drove straight up to the hospital to be by your bedside. You have to believe me … the reason I met with her that night was to break it off with her.

I told her I wasn't leaving you. I told her you were pregnant with our child. But she wouldn't accept the breakup. She got so angry. She was threatening to tell that I'd conceived a son with her. Not long after she said that, your car hit us. I looked over to her and I just ... panicked . . ." His voice trails off. "She was dying, and—"

"And you thought it was better to just let her die ... didn't you, Jonathan? You thought I wouldn't find out about your love child with her if she was dead. You thought you could get away with it. All of it."

"There was nothing I could do for her," he says, pouring himself another scotch with shaking hands. He looks at me. His eyes are glassy and pleading.

"Liar! No wonder you're a brilliant lawyer; you lie so well," I snarl. "You left the scene of a fatal accident. How could you?! I'm telling the police that you left us there to die," I say as I walk toward the hallway.

He's suddenly in my face, blocking my path.

"No, you're not; they won't believe you. They won't believe a woman with amnesia. They will think *you* are crazy," he says, grabbing my face in his hands. He pushes me back against the kitchen counter with his body as he grabs my face harder between his hands; his fingernails dig into the flesh of my cheeks. He lifts my head up higher and backward.

"Let go. Let go of me," I whisper, trying to find my voice.

My eyes look up to his, pleading. But his are dark voids. He tightens his grip around my head with both hands.

I reach up and place one hand on his, trying to release his grasp, and with my other hand, I reach behind, hoping the knife is still where I'd left it on the counter. One of my fingers can just reach the tip of the handle, and I guide it closer so I can grab it.

"Let her go, Jonathan!" a familiar voice demands from behind him.

But it's too late. I've already swung, and I plow the knife hard into his shoulder. He stumbles backward, wide-eyed, as he falls silently to his knees. His eyes are fixed, locked onto mine.

He has a look of disbelief, as if *he's* the one who has been betrayed.

Blood pools through his white shirt, and a lone tear rolls down his cheek. But I know now it's not a tear for me, Mia, Charlie, or the baby we lost. It's a tear for himself.

I look up to see Brianna standing at the entrance of the kitchen, white-faced.

"I've got it all on tape," she says to Jonathan, holding up her cell phone. "I heard it all. Don't you dare move!" she bellows at him with a pointed finger.

He lets out a faint groan as he falls flat on his back on the kitchen floor.

"The police are already on their way," she says, rushing to my side. She wraps her arms around me. "I'll call an ambulance."

* * *

CHAPTER THIRTY-ONE

MIA

June 15th, 2012
New York
Morning

I wake to the sound of his cries and get up out of bed to go to him. I open the blinds in his room, pick him up out of his crib, and hold him close to my chest to soothe him.

The summer sun has arrived, and its light filters into his room. He settles quickly in my arms as I carry him over to the warmth of the window. The weather reports said it was going to be hot this morning, with a severe thunderstorm and heavy winds and rain this afternoon. As I rock him in my arms, I take in the view from my Manhattan apartment.

I see people going about their business, the joggers in Central Park enjoying the bright morning while it lasts, and I wonder if they are happy like I am. Before he was born in November, I'd never felt such unconditional love. For the first time in a long while, I've found my happiness with him. A purpose. I coo at him and kiss him softly on his forehead.

I look at his clock. It's 7:30 a.m. The nanny will arrive soon, and I must get ready for work. I carry him back to my bedroom and place him on the rug on the floor. I watch him closely and talk to him as I get dressed.

My cell phone vibrates on the bedside table. It's a text from Jonathan.

Mia, I can't do this anymore. I want to make my marriage work. I'm sorry. J.

What?! *Please, no.* He promised me he would leave her. I text him back. *What do you mean?*

There is no reply after five minutes, so I text him again.

Can we talk about this? Please! M.

He responds promptly. *I'm working late. Pick me up outside my office at eight-thirty.*

Oh, thank god. *OK. Love you.*

I call the nanny and let her know I will need her to work late tonight.

* * *

299

June 15th, 2012
Evening

The severe weather has arrived as predicted; it's raining heavily and windy. The streets of New York City are unusually dark and quiet for this time of night. Everyone is staying inside to avoid the storm. It's eerie. I pull up outside Jonathan's office. He's waiting on the pavement with a black umbrella. I smile up at him from the car, but he doesn't return the smile; his face is devoid of expression. I lean over to open the passenger door for him as he closes his umbrella.

"Hi," I say when he gets in. He flinches when I kiss him on the cheek, and he won't look me in the eye. He clenches his jaw; he's extremely tense. *Oh no. He's giving me the silent treatment.*

"Where to?" I ask in an upbeat voice.

"Just drive. Head toward Prospect Park. We need to talk." His tone is serious as he points ahead.

"Jonathan, what's going on?" I ask, twirling the hair on the nape of his neck. He pushes my hand away.

"What's wrong?" I ask him, perplexed. Finally, he turns in his seat to look at me.

"It's over between us. I want to make it work with Anouk."

"Are you fucking serious, Jonathan? She was sleeping with Tom, for heaven's sake. She doesn't love you like I love you."

"She broke it off with Tom ages ago. She wants to make it work with me, and I want to make it work with her."

"Please, Jonathan. Don't do this. I love you."

"She's pregnant, Mia, with my child. She's twenty weeks along," he blurts out.

"What? Bullshit!" *No. No. She can't do this. She had her chance with him.* "Don't believe her, Jonathan. It's probably Tom's baby. She's lying."

"It's my baby. The dates work out," he says.

Why didn't she tell me? "No! She's lying," I protest. "She doesn't want kids. She'd make a terrible mother."

"She wants this baby; she's happy about the pregnancy. She's changed, and I want my marriage to work. You know this is what I always wanted." He doesn't look at me when he says it. He's looking straight ahead, his eyes fixed on the road.

"What about me? I'm the mother of your child. You promised me you would leave her! What about Charlie?" I shout. "She was unfaithful to you, and she'll do it again."

"And I was unfaithful to her with *you*. I want to make things right in my marriage, Mia. Look, I'm sorry. I'll still look after you and Charlie financially. I'll pay child support, of course."

Sorry? He's sorry? He promised me that he was going to leave her. I feel a sob rise in my throat. The thought of losing him is just too much for me to bear. I can't imagine my life with him not in it. My shock and hurt quickly turn into anger. I'm now filled with rage. *I won't be discarded.* I accelerate hard through the wet streets.

"You're sorry?" I scoff. "No. I won't let it be over. It's not over. Don't say that."

"It's over, Mia. You're acting crazy."

"No. You're mine."

"Slow down. You're being irrational. Take me back to my office to get my car. I want to go home. Now!"

"No. I'm going to take you home, and I'm going to tell her about us, that we're in love. I'm going to tell her you have a child with *me*." I accelerate hard, taking a left turn to head toward his apartment.

"No, Mia. I'm going to tell her anyway. I'm going to tell her the truth."

"She can't have you. She doesn't deserve you." I accelerate harder. The rain is pounding the windshield.

"Please, Mia," he says, grabbing at the steering wheel. "You're going too fast."

I won't let him leave me. I grab his head with one hand and push his lips onto mine. I hold his head locked hard onto my lips. My eyes aren't on the road, but I don't care.

"Let go," he murmurs, trying to get out of my grasp. His tone is angry.

He turns the steering wheel to bring the car back into the center of the road. I let go of him, push his hand off the steering wheel, and accelerate harder.

"Enough, Mia. Please!"

"No. She will never have you." *I've made sure of that.*

"Slow down!" he orders. I take my foot off the accelerator to brake.

Boom! A metallic bang vibrates from the back of the car, throwing our heads violently back onto our seats. I'm disoriented; it's hard to see through the rain on the windshield. *What hit us? What's happened?* I glance over at Jonathan. He's dazed, rubbing the back of his neck.

"Look out!" he says, grabbing at the wheel.

I brake, but it's no use. The car careens and glides at full speed diagonally toward the curb. *Oh no.* I can't control the steering, and the car is rushing toward a lamppost. Jonathan grabs the wheel in desperation, trying to keep us on the road.

"Brake!" he yells.

"Jonathan!"

* * *

June 15th, 2012
Afternoon

I'll show *her*. That bitch. I gave him something that she would never give him. A son. She was just too damned selfish. If she thinks she can take anything she wants, she's wrong. I hate her—hate her with a passion.

All these years, she's taken credit for my designs and pocketed the profits from *my* sweat and labor. She used me. She stole from me, so I'll steal from her. Jonathan is mine.

I slide on a pair of gloves as I exit the elevator in the basement. It's mid-afternoon, and she's in a monthly meeting, so I must be quick. I can't see any movement in the parking lot as I approach the Corvette.

A couple of cars drive in my direction toward the exit.

Someone might see me. I slide under the Corvette, bumping my head on the car's frame, and a few strands of my hair get caught on something. *Shit!* I pull the small flashlight and pliers out of the pocket of my pantsuit. I see the brake line. *At least that filthy pig of a man taught me something.* There, it's done.

And she had it coming.

She won't know. He won't know.

* * *

CHAPTER THIRTY-TWO

ANOUK

June 21st, 2014
Morning

Jonathan made a full recovery. The knife had narrowly missed an artery, luckily for him. Brianna testified as a witness against Jonathan when I went to court, and it was ruled an act of self-defense.

He tried to call me numerous times after the incident, but I didn't answer. Jonathan confessed everything to Detective Mantle while he was in the hospital; he'd made a deal with Bob, or more accurately, he'd blackmailed Bob so that he could raise Charlie in exchange for not going to the police to report the abuse Mia had suffered at Bob's hands. Mia had confided in Jonathan.

Bob had to keep quiet about it and not contest custody as part of the deal. Once Jonathan was told by the doctors I had amnesia, it was easy then for him to fool me into believing Charlie was mine.

The truth came out in court, and Charlie's death was ruled an accident. Jonathan had his lawyer call a surprise witness: Lauren. She cried on the witness stand as she recalled how she'd come to our house that fateful day to talk to Jonathan about a work-related matter. He was hungover and distracted, on a phone call to a client, when he answered the door. She saw Charlie at the top of the stairs behind him—and she saw Charlie fall.

"It happened so quickly," she sobbed. They had tried desperately to save him. Lauren admitted under questioning that she had visited our house numerous times when she was out jogging. She hesitantly confessed that she was still in love with Jonathan after all these years. But she swore adamantly that she meant no harm to any of us, most of all Charlie. She was envious of the life I had with Jonathan and said she would sometimes watch me through our window, wishing that she was his wife.

Jonathan had lied, even though he didn't have to. It had become second nature to him. At least he had the decency to give our baby a proper burial as I lay unaware of my loss in the hospital. I visit his grave often, at a little cemetery just outside the city. I have since had a headstone made to mark his resting place. And I named him after my father, Noah.

The medical documents were released in court. A hospital representative testified that there was little that Jonathan or they could have done to save Noah that rainy night. And I was lucky to have survived at all.

Jonathan is still practicing law, even though he'd been charged with felony assault. Brianna said Ewan must have pulled a few strings with his connections to keep everything that happened quiet. That's Brianna's take. Ewan had the contacts, including the chief prosecutor and Mayor Caldwell. Jonathan protested in court that he left the scene of the car accident to get help because his and Mia's cell phones were damaged. The jury bought it, even though he gave false statements and lied to the police about not being a passenger in Mia's car that night and left out that Lauren was a witness to Charlie's fall. His excuse in court was that he didn't want me to know he *was* sleeping with Mia and for me to think he was sleeping with Lauren. He didn't want to destroy his marriage. He said he loved me deeply, but I was "a jealous type." He was eventually sentenced to house arrest; five months of electronic monitoring, and he is not allowed to contact or approach me again.

After everything that happened, I had to leave Atlanta.

Jonathan stayed in the dream house in Atlanta when he was released from the hospital, and there were no surprises when Brianna told me that Lauren moved in with Jonathan after he was sentenced. It still hurts when I think of them in that house.

Brianna said that Lauren swore to her recently that her relationship with Jonathan only started after I moved to New York. Lauren had left James without warning, and Brianna said James was a broken man when she saw him downtown not long afterward. Brianna made the decision then that she would distance herself completely from Lauren. She was disgusted that Lauren never went to the police nor said anything to anyone after witnessing Charlie's fall. For Brianna, it was an unforgivable act.

In the end, I signed over the house in Atlanta to Jonathan. I didn't want it; I wanted to forget. Brianna recommended an excellent divorce lawyer who helped me get a relatively quick divorce. I had enough money to buy an apartment in New York; Jonathan hadn't touched my bank accounts the whole time we were married. With everything that he'd done, money had not been the motive.

Detective Mantle was able to obtain Patricia's permission, just before she passed, to exhume Mia's remains and get DNA. He later confirmed the DNA was a positive match to the DNA found under the

Corvette. The case was closed. Ironically, when Mia cut my brakes, she'd sealed her own fate.

Detective Mantle, Brianna, and I are trying to bring Bob to justice for what he did to Mia. It's the least I can do for her after the way I treated her over the years, even though she tried to kill me. I take comfort in the fact that I loved her son as my own.

Mia used me, and I used her. I gave her a way out of her past, and in return, she gave me a gift: a son. Charlie brought out the best in me. I'm a better person for being his mother. I believe it was my destiny to look after him and that Mia's and my paths were meant to cross; kindred spirits, I suppose.

I contacted my parents when I got back to New York. They welcomed me with open arms when I turned up at their door. My mother held me tightly in her arms for a very long time when she saw me. I'm a lot like her. I talked to them for hours and told them *everything* that had happened. And they did want a relationship with me after all.

It turned out that I had cut them out of my life after they gave me the money to set up the fashion house. *I* didn't invite them to my wedding. *I* was the one who had treated *them* poorly. Mia's diary entries confirmed it: They weren't bad parents, just preoccupied, and I was spoiled and self-centered. Jonathan played on this fact, and it made it easy for him to persuade me to move to Atlanta with him. Thankfully, my parents forgive me. They love me.

Jonathan told Detective Mantle that despite his resentment of Tom, he'd promoted Tom to CEO shortly after my accident to allow us to move to Atlanta relatively quickly without impacting my business. Jonathan said he knew Tom was ambitious and that Tom would then focus on the business instead of me.

I still haven't gotten all of my memory back, but I don't mind; I want to forget the past. But I will never forget Charlie and Noah. I went back to work, and I'm now working with Chloe, Alison, and Tom on finalizing the designs for a line of baby clothes. I've hired James to take the photos for the upcoming children's catalog. It seemed like the right thing to do after Lauren had left. I felt for him.

I pick up the framed photo of Charlie from the bookshelf; it's the photo of him as a newborn that used to sit on my bedside table in Atlanta. I have since cut Jonathan out. And I now know that Mia took the photo.

I chose to forgive Mia after I read all her diaries. Tom came with me when I went to Philadelphia one weekend soon after the incident. I had to go, to pay my final respects and lay flowers where she's buried. Mia, like all of us, just wanted to be loved. Although she resented me, and rightly so, I know she once cared for me too. And her talent was the reason the fashion house is so successful.

I pull Charlie's lock of hair out of my pocket and massage it gently, stroking it between my fingers. I had given some of the strands to Detective Mantle for the DNA analysis. I haven't seen Detective Mantle in a while, but he calls me every now and then. The last time we spoke, he told me that his wife was pregnant with their first child. To say he's excited is an understatement.

I've chosen to forgive and forget Jonathan too; however, I would have given anything to have been there to see the look on his face when Detective Mantle told him that Charlie wasn't his biological child after all. DNA testing confirmed that Charlie was Johann's and Mia's baby. Detective Mantle said Jonathan howled and fell to his knees when he got the news. Mia had betrayed him. The news was bittersweet.

I felt sad for Ewan and Claire.

Johann and his mother, Ada, took the news of Charlie's death hard after they found out his paternity. Ada said she would have fully supported Johann in raising him if she had known.

I keep in regular contact with Brianna. She and Eric are coming to stay with me in a couple of weeks for the Fourth of July celebrations. Brianna doesn't know it yet, but I'm going to ask her to be my baby's godmother. Leanne is hoping to visit next month with Emily, too.

I can feel the warmth of Tom's breath on the back of my neck. He wraps his arms around me and gently pats my growing belly as I look out of the floor-to-ceiling windows of our new apartment.

"Happy to be back in New York?" he asks in an upbeat voice.

"Yes. A fresh start," I breathe.

"I'm happy anywhere, as long as I'm with you and our son."

I smile and place my hand over his on my belly and turn to kiss him on the mouth. He gives me a broad smile, and I relax my head back onto his shoulder and take in a deep breath of contentment. I'm happy. I take a mental picture of us in this moment, looking out over the New York City skyline.

I will remember us in this moment—always.

ACKNOWLEDGMENTS

This story is partially inspired by my sister Jane's brain cancer diagnosis at the age of 37, her subsequent surgeries, and her recovery. While this novel is a work of fiction, I have captured within it some of her real-life physical challenges and amnesia as she continued to mother two young sons. It was her journey toward recovery and her courage that inspired me to write. This novel is for her and is my debut as an author.

Thank you to my husband and children for your support, love, and allowing me the space to write over the past five years. You are my life.

To my parents, thank you for raising me to believe I can do anything I put my mind to.

And to the reader, thank you for reading. I hope you enjoyed this story. If so, your review means so much.